Eagle Mountain

A Coal Country Novel

HILLARY DEVISSER

Eagle Mountain

one

"MARIE, IT'S OKAY TO BE SAD."

She outwardly winced and looked at her therapist. "I know that."

"Do you? You seem to be having a rough time allowing yourself to acknowledge that you cared for David."

Marie sighed and felt her face take on the expression that used to get her smacked as a teenager. "He screwed me over."

Dr. Klein shrugged a narrow shoulder. "Yes, he screwed you over, but up until the moment he did, you cared for him."

A shiver ran down her spine. Marie didn't do feelings. Not for people that didn't deserve them, anyway. "Maybe, but all that was over once I found out what he did."

"Look, you don't pay me to blow smoke up your rear end. You cared for him. That's why it hurt when you found out about his betrayal," Dr. Klein said, his frank expression boring into Marie's brain.

She threw an exaggerated hand in the air. "Fine. I cared for him. But what he did was incomprehensible," she said, hating the emotion in her own voice.

Dr. Klein nodded his head in agreement. "It's true. You were humiliated; I get that. Here's the thing, Marie. David was out to get reviews. He wanted to create hype. Was he selfless in the relationship? Is this a big change for him to put his own needs first?"

An unladylike snort erupted from her lips. "Not hardly."

"Okay then, so we agree on a few things. He outed you to stir the pot and gain readership. He clearly didn't give two squirts if he exploited you in the process, pardon my French," Dr. Klein said with a shrug. "So, if he's a waste of oxygen, why are you still giving him power over you?" He quirked an eyebrow as he waited for Marie to push through her building rage before she hammered him with a reply.

She heaved a breath intended to calm her anger. "What are you getting at, exactly?"

"What's done is done. He kept his job. He grew his column readership. He racked up publicity. You're sitting here rehashing something that happened six months ago—reacting, rather than acting."

"What do you want me to do? Act on my impulse to burn his house down?"

"Eh, no, Marie. I'm clearly not pushing for that. What I do want you to focus on now is what is next for you." Dr. Klein paused and adjusted his glasses. "What are you going to do to move past this moment and continue moving forward?" He watched Marie as she resettled herself in her seat, fidgeting as she had been throughout the entire session.

Adjusting the hem of her shirt in her lap for the thousandth time, she looked up into Dr. Klein's kind eyes and said, "I'm going to get out of town."

A smile of surprise danced across his face. "Interesting idea. What will you do?"

She shrugged a shoulder. "I'm not sure. I need a change of scenery. This city feels like it's suffocating me. Everywhere I go I feel like too many people recognize me as the woman in his article. I want to go someplace where I'm not a punchline."

Dr. Klein muttered noises of agreement as he made a note on the notepad balanced on the arm of his chair. "Where to?"

Marie leaned forward and rested her head in her hands as her fingers rubbed her temples. "I think I know just the place. I've got a friend in southern Illinois that I'm going to reach out to. It's secluded, relaxed, and beautiful. Everything I'm not right now."

"Marie," Dr. Klein said with a pause as he stood to walk her to the door. "You are still the same magnificent person you were before David published that article. He didn't change you. He was out to get attention without regard to how it affected you. Don't let him rob you of your self-worth. You've worked too hard to get it back."

A hot tear crested and ran down her face. She wiped at it, annoyed that her body was even capable of creating more tears. "Thank you, Dr. Klein. I've got some vacation time to burn. I should be back in a month or so."

"Take care, Marie. You will push through this," he answered with a kind and reassuring smile. "You've got my number if you need me."

A new layer of steel formed at her spine, and Marie decided Dr. Klein was on to something. She was intelligent and wise. She didn't need David or anyone else to engineer her happiness. She'd been single for over a decade with just a few scant relationships to even consider during her adult life. She preferred it that way, especially in her early forties when everyone seemed to have a heap of children and at least one mildly psychotic ex to contend with. A huff of laughter escaped her at that thought. As she walked to her car in the parking lot, Marie thumbed Jesse's number into her phone. Man, she missed her work wife. They'd been inseparable while Jesse had worked in-office. Now Jesse telecommuted, and Marie rarely got the chance to hug her neck, or hear her big, horsey laugh in person. They'd been their own version of Thelma and Louise, plus the crappy husband, but minus the cliff-diving convertible.

Dependable as ever, Jesse answered directly.

"Jesse?"

"Hey, Marie, so nice to hear your voice! It's been a few months."

A small smile quirked on Marie's face at the sound of her friend's voice. Jesse had reclaimed the slightly Southern accent she'd tried so hard to drop while she lived and worked in St. Louis. It suited her beautifully. "I need a break from the city. I'm going to take a leave of absence. Do you know of any cabins down your way that I could rent for a month or so? Something with a pretty view?"

Jesse paused before answering. "Yeah, there are cabins about an hour away down on the riverfront. They're gorgeous. Are you sure, though? You're not very… well, you're not very nature-y."

Marie let out a long sigh. "I know. I just need out of here for a little while. Can you get me the contact info for the cabins please?

"You bet. I'll get the number to you right away. I can't wait to see you. Bye, Marie."

"Thanks, Jesse." Marie locked her car door and eased her head back against the seat. Maybe a change would help her get past this idiocy. She could pawn her current leads off to a few coworkers easily enough. God knows people in sales were always open to fresh blood. Especially if it concerned new territory. She dialed her boss's phone number as she switched her phone to Bluetooth and coasted toward the interstate that would take her to her now half-empty apartment. If she was going to throw a pity party—and hopefully get the hell over it—she could at least do it in a swanky little cabin overlooking the Ohio River.

two

I'm literally in the middle of nowhere. - Marie

What? Not your style? I told you you were definitely more city than country. Quit texting and driving! - HC

Yeah, yeah. Love you. - Marie

Love you. - HC

MARIE MENTALLY SHAMED HERSELF for texting while driving and put the phone down. "What made me think this would be a good idea? There's probably freaking werewolves hunkered down in the bushes over there," Marie muttered aloud, squinting out the window of her sleek sedan. "Go live in the woods in the middle of the freaking winter. Great idea, Marie." She drove farther up the hill and allowed herself to think about her idiotic decision to escape her situation in St. Louis and live in the wilderness for a few months.

Another empty field came and went. "Sabbatical my butt," she hissed as she double checked the directions to her cabin for the thirty-fifth time since crossing the Mississippi. "What am I? Some kind of fancy-pants college professor?" She turned right at one of the street signs that looked so foreign out in the middle of nowhere. Did people really live out in the country like this? How did they stand it? She prayed she was headed the right direction and absently wondered how long she'd have to drive to find out she wasn't. Her heater was steaming up the windshield, so she pulled to the side of the road to crack the window and let the air circulate a bit so that she could stand a chance of seeing the gravel road.

Before she even had a chance to crack the window, bright lights appeared in the rearview mirror. Marie's blood ran cold at the sight. It had taken her nearly forty-five minutes to get used to being the only person on the road, and suddenly, where she'd have been comforted by the sight of another driver in the city, the sight made her hair stand on end far out in the country like she was. *Who the hell is out in the middle of the night?* she asked herself and flinched when the clock revealed it was only 7:00 PM. Admittedly, it was certainly darker in this area. Not a street light to be found for miles. There were, however, stars as far as the eye could see. Something skittered out across her headlights, and she half-watched it while tracking the bright lights rumbling up behind her. *What even was that?* she asked herself, face wrinkling in disgust at whatever wild animal had just zipped across the road in front of her car. An engine roared to life behind her, pausing with a deep rumble outside her window. Marie felt for the pepper spray in her purse as the stranger's truck idled beside her car.

She cracked the window when she realized the driver had rolled his down. She couldn't see anything, but she heard a deep voice petition a question.

"Hey, ya doing alright over there? Got a flat or somethin'?" a man called out to her before the unmistakable spit-sound of chewing tobacco being hawked out the window made it to her ears.

"Fine!" she shrieked, annoyed at the sound of her own voice. She rode the MetroLink. She walked most parts of St. Louis without flinching. She wasn't going to let some hillbilly scare the crap out of her. "Thank you," she yelled before frantically rolling up her window and double checking that her doors were locked.

She scowled when she heard a low chuckle respond to her words. "Okay, then. Have a good night, *ma'am*," he added. Marie had the distinct feeling it was more of a dig than a perfunctory salutation.

"Ma'am," she said aloud, rolling her eyes. *Come on*, she thought. *We're not in the deep South. What's with the pukey politeness here?* She recoiled a little at her own pissiness. She'd been initially surprised when she stopped at the grocery store in her friend's town to shop for supplies. A grocery store bagger actually asked if she'd like help with a carryout. She'd never had that experience in her whole life, though she remembered her mother telling her about how things used to be in "the good old days" when she'd been growing up in the outskirts of a metropolitan area. Same thing happened when she pulled up to an automatic car wash. She'd treated the attendant like he was a potential robber when he stood beside the kiosk and asked which wash she'd like as he took her cash and fed it to the machine. She realized she'd become a little weird about human interaction from her time in the city.

So what if she automatically locked her car doors the instant she got in her vehicle, or if she locked her house when she stepped outside to water the plants? You never knew when some creep was going to try and get into your space. What's the harm in being prepared? Her mother had often teased her for being overly cautious, but then again, the world had been a bit different when her mother had grown up. That's when a person could safely hitchhike across the country without ending up the subject of a milk carton or a late night, horror-inducing TV special.

Marie was all about precautions. She checked again that her window was rolled up after watching with relief as the huge truck rumbled in front of her car along the gravel road. What was it with rural folk and growling engines? Okay, fine. She wouldn't lie. The big, roaring truck was kind of hot. She briefly allowed herself to imagine some golden-haired god, with biceps like tree trunks, man-handling the big truck. As petite as she was, a man didn't have to be very big to tower over her. Marie didn't have an alpha male fetish, but she did appreciate a nice specimen here and there. Though she didn't have a dyed-in-the-wool physical type that she was attracted to, a man did need to be clean-cut, well-travelled, and smart as a tack to ruffle her feathers.

The fog had cleared from her window, and she pulled back onto the road. Marie let her mind linger on the sexy man daydream until her body recoiled against the path her mind had taken. The reason she was out in the wilderness right now was because she'd had her fill of men. One in particular. She wasn't going to let herself go there right now. She reminded herself she had the huge moon to appreciate, the crunch of the gravel to lull her into relaxation, and the huge white owl flying low across the front of her car to dodge.

What in the actual hell? Marie smashed the brakes to avoid the enormous bird, and her tires left the road. She tried to right her mistake and overcorrected, sending her car fishtailing on the loose gravel into a ditch. The car tilted alarmingly to the right and stopped with a scrape and thud.

"No!" Marie yelled, quickly shutting off the engine. Tears of fear, annoyance, and utter rage filled her eyes as she fought back the waves of stress that had been building and building beneath the surface for the last several months. Unwilling to break even a little bit at the moment, she wiped them away hastily.

Marie rubbed the side of her head where it had whacked the window and checked herself to make certain nothing was broken aside from the stupid, traitorous car. She threw the door open, heels struggling for purchase in the lightly snow-covered ground as she climbed out of the car. Thank God the ditch wasn't deeper than it was. However, there was no way she'd ever back out on her own. She was going to need a tow truck. The curses pouring from her mouth might be dirty enough to make a sailor blush.

She climbed back into the car, retrieved her purse from the floorboard, and fished around until she found her phone, which had zero battery life. "Perfect. Great idea, Marie. Rent a cabin out in the boonies, and see what the world hands you? A car wreck." She stomped around to the trunk and pulled out the winter coat she'd brought along. Wrapping herself up in her heavy coat, she took a deep breath to steady her nerves. She wished she'd brought warmer or even sensible shoes, but hiking hadn't been on the itinerary since it was the middle of winter. She was five foot nothing and lived in heels.

Marie steeled herself against her situation, wrapped her coat up tight, pulled her directions to the cabin she'd rented, and decided she'd be fine. She freaking dared a Sasquatch to come out of the trees and mess with her. Her pepper spray was tucked away in her open purse, and her badass attitude was on full tilt.

"I'll be fine. The cabin is just up the road," she told herself aloud. Half a mile into her walk, she stopped to check her directions again, certain the turn was coming soon. Marie's hair stood on end when a truck rumbled up the road. She stepped to the side to avoid being run over by what was surely a Neanderthal given the roar of the engine on that thing. The truck slowed beside her as the lights switched from high- to low-beam.

"Ma'am, can I help you?"

Again with the ma'am, Jesus H... "I'm fine, thanks," she said, anxiety and exasperation seeping from every pore of her body.

"Can I give you a lift somewhere?" the stranger asked, his voice a low rumble that tickled her ear.

Fear spiked within Marie, and she realized bravado wouldn't be enough to protect her at this point. Her hand instinctively patted the pepper spray in her purse for reassurance as she answered. "No thanks, I'm nearly where I'm supposed to be, thank you. Good night," she said, resuming her walk and dismissing whomever it was that wasn't taking the hint that she was done talking.

Rather than driving on, the stranger asked, "You wouldn't be Marie Capello, would you?

Her head snapped toward him at that. "Yes, and just who the hell are you?" she asked, turning on her heel and planting her hand on her hip, attitude masking her nerves.

"Well, ma'am, I'm Cole Green, and my friend, Ryan Dade, owns the cabin you've rented. It was pretty easy to guess who you are. Not a whole lot of unfamiliar traffic out in these parts. You alright, Ms. Capello? I saw a car in the ditch."

Flustered, Marie ran a hand across her coat, smoothing

imaginary wrinkles from it. "I'm fine. Just ready to get to the cabin."

"I'd be happy to give you a lift. It's just a mile or so up the road," the stranger said, flicking on the interior light of his truck.

She sucked in her breath at the sight of the man staring down at her. He reached across the cab of the truck and held the door open for her. Marie quickly weighed her options. She was out in the literal middle of nowhere. She didn't know where she was going. This dude knew her name, which meant there was a good chance he actually did know Mr. Dade and likely wasn't a serial killer. The night was growing impossibly darker, and no phone reception was to be found—well, she assumed so, anyway, seeing as how her phone battery was dead. Marie did what she never did. She admitted defeat.

"Thank you," she said, approaching his truck.

Cole watched her look around as she tried to figure out how to get into the behemoth of a truck. He extended his hand to her to help haul her up.

Discomfort radiated from Marie, but there was nothing else to grab onto. She placed her hand in his and marveled at the difference in size as the man easily balanced pulling her up and bracing his arm so that she could do most of the work herself. *I have control issues, so what?* she asked herself and pulled a face when she saw his grin.

"You have more stuff to bring, or are you roughing it with whatever's in that little purse of yours?"

"Excuse me?" she asked leveling her eyes on the man who seemed to eat up all the available air in the cab of the truck.

Cole took a deep breath and spoke as if he were dealing with a simpleton. "Well, you're here, and your car is back a ways. Do you have more luggage you'd like to gather before you go to Ryan's cabin for the evening? If so, I'll swing back and get it."

She inhaled through her nose and let the breath exit her mouth in a slow exhale. "That would be very nice, thank you." Marie fidgeted and pressed her hands to her lap when she noticed for the first time that her hands were shaking.

Cole studied the terrified little woman a second to be sure she'd buckled up. He put his arm across the back of the truck seat before putting the truck into gear, and Marie flinched as if he'd tried to slap her. She jerked her face toward the window, and he heard her pull in a long breath and release it slowly.

He intentionally masked his reaction and unfurrowed his brow as he looked behind him and did a three-point turn while making sure not to brush his fingers against her shoulder. Cole had only ever seen one other woman flinch and jerk away from a man's touch before. He closed his mind against childhood memories of his mother with a busted lip or a black eye. This was the first time a woman had ever jerked away from him, and it twisted his gut to think of what she must've experienced to react like that.

Maybe she was just freaked out about the circumstance. They were well up Eagle Mountain, and she'd run her car into a ditch. It was darker than a coal miner's lunch bucket outside. She clearly wasn't dressed for a hike, and her empty car had been about half a mile back from where he'd seen her walking. *She had a right to be on edge*, he told himself, wanting to ease his own mind. She remained silent as his truck ate up the gravel road.

When they approached her car parked on the side of the road, he stepped out and walked to the trunk as Marie thumbed the button on the key fob that she had fished from her purse.

"Anything else you'd like me to get?" Cole asked, keeping his distance from her unrolled window.

She scrunched her face up in what she probably thought passed as a half smile. "No. And, thank you so much. My manners…" She sighed with a slight shake of her head. "What was your name again, please?"

He gently placed her fancy luggage in the bed of his truck. "I'm Cole Green. Nice to meet you," he said, extending his hand.

Marie took his hand and did her best to disguise the jolt of electricity that shot from her hand to her toes at his touch. This guy was not her type. First, he was enormous. Second, he had a beard that made him look like a wildman. Dude had a truck that nearly took a step ladder to climb into, and it was loud. Marie liked lawyers, not lumberjacks. "Nice to meet you, too," she stammered. "Thank you for giving me a ride," she added, cringing once the words left her lips.

Cole smirked and shifted his truck into gear, turning

back toward their original direction. "We'll be at the cabin soon. I'll make sure and get you the number for a tow truck if Ryan doesn't beat me to it."

"Thanks. Do you live out this way?" she asked, deciding polite conversation was the way to go. There was no reason to be rude. It wasn't his fault she ran into a ditch. She rubbed at the spot between her eyes where she was sure she had a perma-wrinkle from the evening's events alone.

"I do. My place is the next lane up from the cabins. What brings you out this way?" he asked, glancing in her direction.

She bristled. Marie wasn't used to sharing her business, certainly not with strangers. Her eyes shuttered, and she mumbled something noncommittal.

"Ms. Capello, does your head hurt," he asked, his hand ghosting over to lightly rest on her shoulder.

Marie jumped out of her skin and plastered herself against the door of his truck.

Cole spoke, his eyes as round as saucers, "I'm sorry. I didn't mean to scare you. I saw you rubbing your head and wondered if you hit it when you wrecked."

She shook her head. "No, I'm fine. I'm just super freaking uncomfortable right now, to be honest."

A quick laugh erupted from Cole at her honesty and, after a tense beat, Marie laughed a little herself.

"Sorry, I'm absolutely stressed and exhausted," she said, fidgeting with her purse. "I am thankful that you stopped for me, though."

"Sure, what are neighbors for?" he said with a half grin, or what she assumed was a grin beneath that beard.

Marie picked up on a smell she'd overlooked in her near-hysteria. "Have you been at a bonfire or something?" she asked, nearly wrinkling her nose.

"You could say that," Cole answered. The sound of his laugh was like a low rumble. It hit Marie in the belly, and she couldn't deny that she wouldn't mind hearing a sound like that more often. He had an accent, too. Southern, much more so than Jesse's. It was something far from where they were. She quirked an eyebrow, waiting for him to elaborate.

"I just got back from working a forest fire in Tennessee," he said with a shrug. "That explains this," Cole said, running his hand down the beard he was sporting. "It itches like a son of a gun. Can't wait to do away with it."

She smiled. "Ah, so you're a firefighter, not a lumberjack like I initially thought."

"Not really, but I'm a forester and volunteer with the reserve fire department when something big is going down. Good practice and prep in case something ever happens here."

"Yeah," she said, looking out at the trees surrounding them. "This place looks like it could be a tinderbox."

"It can be, in the right conditions. Thankfully, we've been lucky in this area for a long time." Cole gestured to the right. "That's the lane to my house right there. The cabins are just up over the hill."

Her eye roll was nearly audible. "Over the hill? It feels

like we're on top of the world already," Marie said, turning in her seat to try and peek at Cole's property.

A small, husky laugh was his only reply. The sound of the gravel began to quiet, and Cole turned into another road. Marie wasn't joking when she was surprised they could continue climbing upward. She ran her hands down her knees, nervousness vibrating out from her body. Cole's mind swam with questions as he watched her out of the corner of his eye.

She caught her own fidgeting and exhaled deeply. "I don't get nervous," she started. Cole pulled his truck to a stop in front of the cabin office. "I don't get nervous, and I don't make rash decisions, and I don't ever, ever visit places like this," she said, throwing her hands in the air. "I don't even *like* nature. I know a person's not supposed to admit stuff like that, but I don't," she said, her words coming out in a rush.

Cole knew she was spiraling. He was fluent in highly emotional women. His sister still called him on a weekly basis to be talked down from one fit or another. "Ms. Capello," he said quietly, "that's a long list of don'ts." He let his eyes leave hers, and they settled on her lips. "Give us a shot out here," Cole said with a slight nod of his head. "It's been a rough start so far, but don't knock what you haven't really tried."

Marie dragged her eyes from his and straightened her back, embarrassed at the angle she had leaned toward him. The sound of his voice was soothing. Something about the cadence of his accent and low tone made her ears want to hear more. She wasn't a beard man at all, but she wanted to feel Cole's face with her fingers to see if he was soft or scratchy. She removed the lusty fog from her brain with a quick shake of her head.

"Thank you, Mr. Green. I don't think I could have made it the rest of the way in these shoes."

"Hmm," Cole answered, eyeing the high arch of her heels, "I don't know, Ms. Capello. I have a feeling you could do just about anything you put your mind to. And call me Cole, by the way."

She allowed herself a grin. "You can call me Marie. Thank you," she said, turning to open the truck door. By the time she found the latch and pushed the heavy door open, Cole was there ready to help her climb down gracefully. Marie was embarrassed to death to take his hand, but these were her favorite Manolos and she didn't want to twist an ankle hopping down into the gravel below. She ignored the closeness of his body, the hardness of his arm as she touched her hand to him as he guided her down from his truck. She even blocked out the woodsy smell of him that had the hairs on the back of her neck standing on end. Marie managed a wan smile when he shut the door and reached into the bed of his truck to haul out the enormous suitcase that had nearly killed her to load into the trunk of her car. She watched as Cole grabbed a few more things that she had brought along and packed it all as it if were nothing. Marie turned to walk up the walkway and jumped like a shot to see another man standing a few feet away.

"Hey, Dade, found your new tenant just down the road. She's going to need a tow into town. Her car's in a ditch; looks like there's some fender damage." Cole nodded to Marie as he walked up the path carrying the majority of the contents of her car.

Marie extended her hand to the other man, a surprised look on his face. Ryan Dade shook her hand and quirked a look to Cole. "Mr. Dade," she said, wondering if every man in this area was straight off a paper towel ad.

"Call me Ryan. You must be Marie? I'm so sorry you had trouble on your way out. What was it? Deer?"

She shook her head. "Some sort of mutant owl from hell, I think," she said, shifting her purse from one arm to the other. "I've never seen anything like it. The stupid thing flew right at my car."

"Yup, sounds like a mutant owl from hell to me," Cole said in a low voice, barely an inch behind Marie. She sucked in an involuntary breath from the electricity radiating off of him, and she caught his smile as he turned back to Ryan. "Which one is she in, Dade?"

"Number three, thanks," Ryan answered. "Marie, there's just a few forms to fill out here in the office, and then I'll get you settled. You can take a quick look at the place before signing if you like,"

"If you say so, but even if it's a dump, I'm not getting back on that gravel road tonight."

When she saw a flash of offense cross Ryan's features she groaned. "I don't mean it the way it sounded. I'm so sorry.

The pictures online were beautiful. I'm just exhausted and lost my filter, oh, about 30 years ago."

He nodded in response. "I understand. Go have a look, and I'll be in the office," he gestured to the building they had passed a few doors down.

She followed the trail down to the cabin with the light blazing in the window. A few moments more of chastising herself over her traveling shoe choice brought her to a heavy-framed wooden door. Marie gasped at her surroundings. She was no stranger to opulence. One perk of traveling constantly for work and being untethered was that she racked up points and upgraded on her personal vacations. The pictures of the cabins online were nice, but this was a whole new level of surprise.

"I'm going to have to eat some crow," she whispered aloud.

"What's that?" Cole asked, walking over to her.

"I said, I'm going to have to eat some crow. I made a crack about staying for the night even if this place was a dump, and I think I offended Mr. Dade."

"Ryan," he corrected. "And yeah, better kiss up and make nice after that one. He takes a lot of pride in this place, and he makes the best pancakes you'll ever eat. If you tick him off, you might be eating cereal during your stay."

She allowed herself to laugh and looked up at Cole. "Thanks again for helping me."

"Anytime," Cole said with a slight smile. "Listen, I'll make sure he gets you the number for a tow truck. And here's mine," he said as he pressed a piece of paper to her hand. "If you need a ride into town, just get in touch. I've got a week off before I start back up at work and will be around." He took a step backward toward the door. "I put your bags in your bedroom. Enjoy your time here."

"I will. Thanks again." Marie liked the way his eyes crinkled a little when he smiled. He ought to be alarming because of his size and the beard, but he was the opposite. If she were the type to ever trust a man again, she could see herself leaning into him for strength. *Screw that*, she thought. She might lean into him at some point, but it would be for sex, not strength. *Men are liars*, she reminded herself.

three

RYAN POURED ANOTHER STEAMING cup of coffee in Cole's mug. "How much longer are we going to sit here and act like this is normal?"

Cole's eyebrows headed north. "What are you talking about, man? We're just drinking coffee."

"This has never happened in the ten years we've been neighbors. Not since high school can I remember you just stopping by, and that was because cell phones were only for the elite among us," Ryan said with a laugh. "God, we're getting old. Any reason you're all of a sudden feeling neighborly?" Ryan teased. "Maybe one particular five foot nothing reason with dark, curly hair?"

"Asshole," Cole muttered as he shrugged.

Ryan laughed. "Listen, she's hot, I'll give you that," he said. "But, I would leave that one alone. She's got a mouth on her and, frankly, she's kind of bitchy."

Ryan jerked as his wife slapped his shoulder with her dish towel. "Who did you just call bitchy?" Amy asked, her eyes boring into his.

"Listen here, honey. Don't whip into a room and go off half-cocked. You know I'd never be stupid enough to call you bitchy out loud," Ryan said as he brought his cup to his lips to cover a grin.

Her eyes met Cole's, and she rolled them in great exaggeration. "Still, it's an ugly word. What are you two talking about? The rest of my day will be spent with children. Give me some grown-up talk, I'm begging you," she said beseechingly.

"I was telling Cole, here, who all of a sudden is feeling chatty enough to come by for coffee in the morning, that our new tenant seems to be meaner than a striped snake," Ryan said with a roll of his neck. "I think he ought to steer clear of her."

"Ah. Is this because of her snide comment about the cabins when she got here? Give the lady a break. She'd been through the wringer before she hit the door." She dropped down into Ryan's lap and gave him a smooch. "Cole?"

"Yeah?" he answered, a gleam in his eye.

"I love this man, but he can be an idiot. Marie is cute; she seems smart as a tack from what little I've spoken with her. And, she's only here for a few weeks, right?" she asked, directing her question to her husband.

He sighed. "Right."

Amy shrugged a shoulder. "So, perfect. No attachments."

Ryan looked alarmed. "Great, now you're thinking like a man. What happened to all the emotion crap?"

"Babe, we've been married for ten years. Don't tell me you never fantasize about a down-and-dirty weekend with someone else from time to time," she said, yelping when he pinched her rear.

Ryan's mouth gaped open. "I can't believe you just said that! Cole, can you believe she just said that? And here she is, a Sunday School teacher."

Amy laughed. "And…"

"And?" Cole prompted.

"If Ryan here were truly turned off by bitchy women, there's no way we'd have ever hit it off. Then we wouldn't have all this!" she said, turning around gesturing to their happy home. Amy grinned and hopped up, rummaging through the kitchen to start breakfast for their kids as Ryan stood and pushed in his chair.

"Yes, dear," Ryan teased, dipping his lips down to kiss her neck before pulling on his jacket. "I'm about to get on the four wheeler to check the fence in the back pasture. Want to come with me?" he asked, holding Cole's coat out to him.

Accepting it, he thanked Amy for the coffee with a nod as he placed his cup in the sink. "No, I've got an errand to run. You called Murray's to tow Marie's car, right?"

"Yeah, man. Levi's place does good work. You're not going to listen to my advice, are you?" Ryan asked, grabbing his keys from the table.

"Not a bit, Dade. Not a bit. Thanks for the coffee, Amy." Cole gave a nod to Ryan and stepped out into the snowy morning.

"Later, man," Ryan answered as he pulled Amy in for a quick hug.

"You know, I think that's the most I've ever heard Cole talk at one time. I'm not sure I've ever heard him string together more than three words."

Ryan nodded his head, brushing his scruffy cheek against Amy's hair. "I think you're right. Poor guy. Talk about being put through the wringer. That Marie chick's got nothing on him."

Her eyes went wide as she waited for more details.

Ryan shifted uneasily. He wasn't big on trading stories about people. "Remember he came to play poker with me and the guys a few times? One night we got absolutely hammered, and I mean to the point where he couldn't even drive home. Being the good neighbor that I am, I walked him halfway to make sure he didn't end up puking in a ditch or something. The dude was so drunk there's no way he remembers what he told me. You remember he was in the Marines after high school, right? When he got home from a deployment, he wanted to surprise his fiancée. You know, like all those online videos you watch and cry over?"

"Come on, keep talking," she said, tapping his arm.

"Well, he came in and unlocked the door with flowers and the whole nine. His fiancée was playing house with some other dude." Ryan shrugged. "You see how big he is?

He flipped his lid, and the other guy ran for his life. His fiancée screamed and cried and told him it was his fault for leaving her alone all the time, and…"

"Seriously?" Amy asked in disbelief.

"Seriously. Anyway, she stayed and argued with him for a while and left in a crying fit. She painted him as the villain and the reason she was a cheating sack of crap. Well, after she left, she ended up wrapping her car around a tree and got herself killed."

Amy's hand flew to her mouth. "Oh my God, that's awful!"

"Yeah, it is. He cried when he told me about it. They met and got engaged young, super fast right after high school, before he enlisted. From what I remember in high school, he was really quiet. I think his home life was pretty screwed up. He moved here toward the end of high school. Anyway, as if he didn't have enough crap going on already, not to mention whatever he saw in his service, that extra guilt didn't do his personality any favors." Ryan sighed and pulled Amy into his arms.

Amy laid her head on his shoulder and enjoyed his embrace. "I feel so sorry for him now. Before, I just thought he was a little creepy."

"Oh, he's a little odd, for sure. One of the most heavily guarded dudes I've ever known. But, I figure he's earned the right to play his cards close to his vest. There's one thing I want to know more about, though."

"What?" Amy answered.

Ryan narrowed his eyes and leaned his face close to hers. "What about these steamy one-nighter fantasies my wife just informed me she has?" he asked as he reached down to give her butt a squeeze.

"Ah, you know. Just a little variety beyond the routine of laundry, picking up after kids, the usual Wednesday Night Special," she teased in a ho-hum voice.

"What? I thought you made me read that stupid book about the importance of making time for each other and scheduling sex and all that crap?"

"Yeah, yeah. I'd just like to," Amy shrugged a shoulder, "work a little more *time* into our schedule."

"That, I can certainly do. Fantasies aside," he emphasized with a squeeze, "I'm glad we don't have to deal with that cat-and-mouse game anymore. This is better," he said with a grin.

"This is better," she agreed, pointing a teasing smile in his direction. "I'll bet you ten bucks Cole and Marie get naked."

Ryan grinned at his wife as he replayed what a hard-ass Marie had been upon her arrival. "You're on."

four

MARIE POURED ANOTHER CUP of coffee and paced the cabin before settling back down in the big, comfy leather chair. Her eyes drifted to the sun glinting off the riverfront, and she had a total thirty seconds of peace before a stain of embarrassment washed over her.

David. One simple newspaper column had destroyed her confidence and hardwon ability to trust. Nine hundred words had ripped open the fragile scab that had begun to cover her wounded heart. Marie closed her eyes and laid her head on the back of the chair. *How could I be so stupid?* she whispered to herself.

Marie couldn't even think of a man she'd been on more than five dates with over the past decade. She didn't *do* attachments. She did a few fun nights out and an occasional weekend getaway where she'd meet a like-minded man who understood the arrangement. Fun? Yes. Feelings? No.

The phone rang, jarring Marie out of her self-punishing line of thought.

"Hey, Jesse. Sorry I haven't called."

"Morning. I was wondering if I was going to have to truck it up the mountain to come check on you," her dear friend answered.

Marie sighed. "I'm sorry, Jesse. To be honest, I was throwing one hell of a pity party. I didn't want to talk to anyone. Not even you."

Jesse laughed in response. "If there's one thing I've always appreciated about you, Marie, it's that you don't beat around the bush."

Marie chuckled. "Life's too short to be vague."

"Amen to that. What's got you down in the dumps?"

"Men." Marie let out a gusty sigh.

"Whoa! What? Are you dating someone? Like, dating-dating?" Jesse asked, shock in her voice.

A hefty sigh left Marie's lips. "I know. Not my style. Did I ever tell you why I don't typically date?"

Jesse picked back through her memories with Marie. She had shared that she married young. She'd also learned quickly that her husband Kevin had a knack for getting hammered and smacking his hand hard across her face when she had the audacity to question why he'd drunk his paycheck. Friday's money went to rounds for everyone at the bar, not the electric bill or the car payment. "You told me that you married early and that he was a jerk."

Marie laughed. "Yeah, that's the gist. He was a jerk in that he hit me a few times. The first time, we were married around four months. I don't know. I guess the new was starting to wear off. The next time was on our six-month anniversary. I waited until he passed out, then I packed everything I could fit into one suitcase and got the hell out."

"I'm so sorry, Marie. I can't imagine how scary that had to be. Drake was an awful human being to be married to, but he never hit."

"Thank God for that. I'd hate to have to kill him."

"Me, too," Jesse answered.

"The morning after I left, I went and filed for a restraining order and a divorce. I expected to wash my hands of him and never look back once the divorce was finalized."

"Did he fight you on it?" Jesse asked.

"Nope. Not even a little. He had a little piece on the side. He was probably relieved to have me out of the way."

Jesse growled in irritation. "God bless. What is it with men and cheating?"

"Drake, too?"

"Oh yeah. In my case, it seemed to be a blessing. He didn't have the attention span to dicker with me too much over the divorce. He was preoccupied."

"Exactly. Well, Kevin was, until the murder."

Marie heard a coughing fit on the other end of the phone.

"The what?" Jesse sputtered. "Crap. Hang on. I need to

grab a rag to mop up the coffee I just sprayed on the floor."

Marie tapped her finger against the table beside her seat. She hadn't allowed herself to play back over the details in several years. It wasn't easy to dig through the mess.

"Okay, I'm back. What the heck happened?"

"He remarried just a few weeks after our divorce was finalized. Like I said, I was so relieved to be free of the mess, that part didn't bother me much. I moved back home with my parents until I got my feet under me. I started as a receptionist at our company, thrilled to have a paycheck. Anyway, I hadn't heard a thing from him—or about him—for years, until I picked up a newspaper and read that he'd been arrested for murdering his wife."

Jesse sucked in a huge breath. "Marie! My God! He's a psycho?"

"Well, probably. The article said he'd been picked up for domestic abuse several times over the course of their marriage. The last time, he'd been drunk off his ass, as usual. When he hit her, she fell and struck her head on the fireplace hearth. She'd died instantly, and Kevin went to prison for manslaughter." Marie didn't allow herself to think of the whole awful affair because she knew how easily it could have been her life that had ended if she'd stayed in that marriage.

"That's horrible. How sad." A pause settled over the conversation.

Marie ran her hand over her face. "Yeah. It really is. That's the long answer to your question."

"What question?" Jesse asked, puzzled.

"Why I don't date. Seriously date. Or that's why I didn't," Marie answered.

"I'm confused."

Marie let out a long breath. "I broke my own rule. I fell for someone and, of course, it blew up in my face."

"Oh," Jesse replied softly.

"After that catastrophe, I gave up on the idea of a committed relationship. Should've stuck with that mindset."

"What the heck happened?" Jesse asked.

"I went to a fundraising event at the art museum last year, one of those fancy ones where you get dolled up like you're going to prom. I met David, a writer for the paper. Sparks flew. We were together for a year."

"How did I not know this?" Jesse demanded.

"Eh, I don't advertise my business, and you've been a little busy, am I right?"

Jesse smiled as she peeped into the living room. On her wall was a gorgeous family portrait from her wedding. She and Levi, their five kids, parents, and the faces of her family smiled back at her. "Got me there. Anyway, go on."

"We didn't live together officially, but we may as well have. Eventually, he started getting distant, and I started getting pissed. I nearly had a stroke when I opened up the paper and found an article espousing the futility of monogamy."

"What? You mean while you were living together? Unofficially?" Jesse added.

"Yup." Marie sighed. "I had the paper laid out on the dinner table when he got home."

"Oh God," Jesse whispered. Marie was a tiny woman, but her temper was bigger than a house.

"It wasn't pretty. Basically it boiled down to this: he said, 'It's been a year. I feel like if I loved you I'd know by now.'"

Jesse gasped. "No!"

"Yeah. It hurt that he didn't love me, but the worst part was that he didn't even try to be coy or detached in his article. It was basically an open letter to me. He bemoaned everything from having to compromise on weekend plans to adjusting to how a lover squeezed the toothpaste from the middle of the tube instead of the top or bottom."

"You do that?" Jesse asked in mock horror.

"Yeah. I'm an animal," Marie answered.

"That absolutely sucks. I'm so sorry, Marie."

Marie walked back to the coffee maker for one more cup of sanity. "It does. My pride took the biggest hit. We'd been to a ton of functions together with our photos in the paper. You know, he was always trying to get exposure and gain readers. I can't even stand to Google myself because there I am, smiling like an idiot all over St. Louis with that jackass. It was humiliating to know anyone reading his article knew he was talking about me. That's why I had to get the hell out of there for a while."

"I absolutely understand," Jesse replied.

"So, after all that, I've just been trying to decompress. I don't know why I picked a mountain in the middle of nowhere instead of a beach, but it's working out okay." She played back that last sentence and winced. "Sorry. That was a crappy thing to say."

"Hey, it's alright. The reason I like this place is because it's in the middle of nowhere. It's a good incentive for taking a vacation, but also a danged good place to raise the kids," Jesse answered. "Can we get together soon? I'd love to take you out while you're here, or get you to my house to chill out and relax."

Marie flipped over to her calendar that was always present in her line of sight. "I have a call at 1:00 tomorrow for work, but I can come over after that."

"I thought you were off work for a few weeks?" Jesse asked, confused.

"I am. You know the company can't live without me. I'm that good."

"You are that good," Jesse replied. "Listen, I have to go. The twins have requested waffles, and waffles they'll have. It's the reward they get for getting up at a normal hour. The others could sleep all day."

"You're such a good mom, Jess."

"Thanks. Call me tomorrow?"

"I'll call tomorrow." Marie ended the call and put her phone down as it pinged with an alert that David's latest article had been posted. She'd set up the notification system when they were together, but like some sick voyeur, she couldn't make herself look away. It reminded her of they way a person continues to check if a spot is still sore when they hurt themselves. It still hurt.

She clicked the link in the alert to see a picture of David with a long-legged blonde. They were dressed to the nines to attend a local filmmaker's documentary at the Tivoli Theater. Envy filled her as she inspected every pixel of the photo. David's arm was lovingly curved around the woman, and her own hand rested on his at the top of her hip. His body was inverted toward hers, screaming possession.

"Asshole," she breathed.

Marie jumped when her phone rang as she held it. "Hello?" She frowned as she answered.

"Marie? This is Ryan. I wanted to let you know your fender has been repaired and delivered. Keys are under your cabin doormat."

She sighed. "Ryan, thank you so much for helping with the arrangements."

"Consider it part of your vacation experience," he said with a laugh. "Actually, I'd like to pretend it was par for the course with our rental, but first off, not many guests get run off the road by a 'mutant owl from hell,' as you put it, and second, it's not often Cole Green offers to handle towing and repair for an out-of-towner."

"What? I thought I'd be taking care of the invoice tomorrow. What do you mean Cole Green took care of it?" Every indignant bone in her body stiffened at the implication that some man was 'handling' her situation.

Ryan hemmed and hawed a little. "Well, I mean, he offered to pay for the towing and repair, so I passed the information to the guys at the repair shop. I'm guessing that is not what you'd like to have happen by the sound of your voice."

"Well, I don't know Cole Green from Adam and am not in the custom of letting strange men take care of my personal business, so correct, I'd like to take care of this myself."

"Fine by me. I'll call the shop now and give them your number to get things straightened out. Either way, your keys are under your mat. I didn't want to disturb you. Have a good day."

"Thank you, Ryan," she said, willing some of the pissiness from her voice. "Don't shoot the messenger, I know. Sorry. Have a good day." It was Cole Green who took liberties assuming she was in need of a knight in shining armor. *She* was the mother freakin' knight.

five

THE MORE MARIE THOUGHT about Cole taking over her car repairs, the more annoyed she became. *Maybe it was a nice gesture. Maybe he thought she owed him something? Hell, no!*

Marie scampered around the cabin and threw on some clothes and a coat. She jerked her keys from under the mat as she stomped toward her vehicle, now drivable. When she flew down the driveway away from the cabins, she missed seeing Ryan grinning out the door of the rental office.

"He said he was a little further up the ridge," she mumbled as she took in the sleepy, snow-covered countryside. She zoomed up the gravel road, feeling her car wiggle a bit as she went. She wasn't in the mood to fishtail into a ditch again, so she let her foot off the gas as she fumed. Before long, Marie reached a driveway with a mailbox with C. Green on the side. She barely hesitated before pulling in. As she reached the apex of the drive, her breath caught at the sight of a beautiful, modern cabin. It looked like something from one of those annoying TV shows where people wanted a new multi-million-dollar home but couldn't see past carpet or wallpaper that wasn't to their liking.

Marie shrugged her shoulders involuntarily. So what if he wasn't some ignorant, misogynistic hillbilly. Maybe he was a well-intentioned, affluent misogynist. Either way, she didn't appreciate him getting in the middle of her business beyond the drive to her cabin. She sprang out of the car and walked up to his door with her purse slung on her hip. As Marie knocked, her heart lurched to her throat. She was alone on a freaking mountain, banging on some controlling idiot's door.

She froze as she heard footsteps and decided there was no way out but complete feminine outrage. Cole swung the door open wearing a look of utter surprise and nothing but a towel swung low on his hips. "Hey, Marie. I didn't expect to see you."

Marie blustered a minute before answering. She felt a pink heat grow on her cheeks and did her best to look at his close-shaven face instead of the droplets of water dripping from his wet hair to his chest. He had dimples when he smiled. Dimples were her weakness. *Breathe, Marie.* Man, was he handsome. Every egg, past, present, and future, clamored for her to make babies with the mountain man. *Channel the outrage,* she reminded herself. She righted her gaze and managed a tight smile instead of letting her tongue loll out of her head. "Well, I just found out you picked up the tab for my towing and repairs, so I had to touch you. *Get in touch,*" she corrected.

Cole smiled and held the door open. "I hope you don't mind. I wanted to, you know, help out. You looked so out of sorts when I ran upon you on the road. It seemed like the neighborly thing to do."

Marie flinched at the low, sexy rumble of his voice. She was set for battle. She hadn't expected sweetness. Especially not sweetness wrapped in a lush bath towel. She exhaled loudly as she flirted with the idea of ripping off that offending bit of material.

"Want to come in?" he said, grinning at her and clearly oblivious to her state of annoyance. The flush must've thrown him off. It had certainly thrown her off balance. It was like her face was literally on fire. She took a step inside his cabin, sweeping a glance from one end to the other. He had a beautiful home. The only indicator that the house was actually lived in was a stack of novels on an end table near the fire.

Marie stalked in, still a little pissed but curious. "Well, I actually came over here to call you a Neanderthal and tell you I'd take care of my own bill. Now I feel a little bit like a jerk and want to start off with a 'thank you' instead." She rolled her shoulders and jerked a look of annoyance at him as his deep chuckle reached her ears.

How could he be so much bigger than I remembered? Marie tilted her head, taking him in. "You busy? Want me to step back outside or something?" she asked, flicking a hand toward his towel in her typically straightforward approach to life.

"No ma'am," Cole answered with a lightning-fast rise of his eyebrows. "You have a look around, and I'll go get dressed. I've been chopping wood and had to take a shower."

Marie scoffed. "Chopping wood. Of course you were," she muttered quietly. Marie inhaled quickly and shook her head to combat the immediate flood of lust. The man looked like some kind of enormous Greek god, but not the kind with a tiny, grape-leaf covered micropenis like the statues portrayed. He'd had a towel wrapped around his hips, but by God, if she was anything, she was observant. *Well done, you,* she said in silent admiration to Cole.

A few minutes ticked by as Marie drifted toward Cole's bookshelves and explored his reading material. Classics, sci-fi, and an expansive historical non-fiction collection filled his shelves. She pulled out a copy of a book she'd read and enjoyed, and flipped to the title page to find an autograph from the author. She was drooling over the page when Cole reemerged, dressed in jeans and a black, v-neck T-shirt.

"Brokaw, huh?" she said, eyebrows to her hairline.

"*Greatest Generation.* Had to have his autograph on that one." He walked toward her and extended his hand for the book. "I was close with my grandparents. This one felt special, like I was getting the backstory they wouldn't or couldn't talk about."

Marie felt a flame ignite in her belly. *History buff, sexy beast, clearly independent, and rugged. Good grief, it's like an estrogen storm up in here*, she thought. No, no, she was going to focus on her pissed-off-edness. It was much more familiar. Anger was more comfortable.

"That's nice." She rolled her shoulders. "Listen, I am going to take care of the cost of my repairs and towing. Thank you, though. That was a nice gesture."

To her surprise, Cole shrugged. "That's okay with me. I just wanted to do something nice for you. You seemed pretty stressed, and it wasn't a big deal. I just wanted to make a good impression, I guess."

"Impression? What are you talking about?" she said as her hands moved to her hips, her natural position.

"Well," Cole said, taking a few steps, which brought him closer to her body, "I met you. I liked you. I wanted to see more of you. So, I thought this was as good of an excuse as any."

"I hear an awful lot of 'I' statements. Is that an indicator of some kind?" she said with a quirked eyebrow.

"Believe me, I make sure my needs usually come last," he said as the room heated up by a billion degrees. Cole moved his body inches closer to hers as her head tilted slightly to the angle it would take for him to easily kiss her lips. Marie felt the awkwardness rise like a tidal wave.

"That might be," she answered, taking a step backward, "but I can take care of it. My needs, I mean. *The bill.* I can take care of the *bill*," she stuttered. "Thank you," she said, stepping back away from the brush of his lips.

Cole nodded. "You're pretty self-sufficient, aren't you?" he asked.

Marie felt her breath coming in fast gulps as her heart sped up. "Yes," she answered in a breathy voice she didn't recognize.

Cole grinned and stepped a tiny bit closer, hooking his finger through a belt loop on her jeans. "You don't like being handled, do you?"

"Interesting choice of words." She stared into his eyes, deciding they reminded her of the ocean as she shook her head slightly.

"Why don't you let me have a try?" he asked softly as his lips pressed down on hers.

She nearly groaned. Marie couldn't decide which sensation was the strongest—his surprisingly soft lips or the prickles her skin felt in response to his body being pressed against hers. The concoction of his skin, scented with something that was inherently male like woods, jasmine, hot sex, and testosterone, ratcheted every molecule of her body to attention.

Her instincts told her to back off and tell him where he could stick his smarmy caveman approach to kissing, but the other part of her wanted to climb him like a monkey up a tree. Marie did what she rarely did and instead told herself to shut up. Cole pulled her close, melding her body against his. She felt so much of him all at once her brain was ready to short circuit. She gave herself a few minutes to enjoy the heady sensations.

Cole's kiss was so different from David's. David had been all tongue, spit, and aggression. Cole was more of a tease, slow but strong. Good Lord, what would he be like at full throttle? Marie reminded herself that David wasn't sitting home crying into a bottle of craft brew. He was out with some honey-haired Amazon goddess. What would be the harm in climbing a mountain man? A moaning sound escaped her at the thought as his hand curved around to her lower back. Her embarrassment jerked her back to her senses.

Marie tipped her head back and pulled in a breath. "Listen," she said as she patted him on the shoulder in two quick swats like she'd do an acquaintance, not a man who had his tongue down her throat seconds ago. "I'll see you later," she said, backing out of his grip. She felt him hold on a second longer than she'd expected, like he was reluctant to let her go. *Of course, idiot*, she said to herself, *he probably thought he was going to get lucky.* She let her eyes drift down to his lips, enjoying the sensation of being desired by such a delectable man.

Cole exhaled a slow breath. "Okay. I'd like to see you soon, though."

"See me?" she asked, hearing the teasing flirtation in her own voice.

"Yeah. Have you for dinner, or take you out in town. Would you like that?"

Her instant reaction was a hormone spike as nervousness began to burn at the base of her spine. Mentally, Marie shook it off. She was a grown-ass woman. One crap relationship within the last decade wasn't going to tear down what she had taken years to build back up.

Marie kicked herself for becoming such a wimp in the face of her recent issues. She was never one to play the coward or take the easy way out. She forced herself to let the desire she felt so completely shine in her eyes. "Sure. I'm free tomorrow night. Does that work for you?"

Cole smiled. "How do you like steak and potatoes?"

Marie scoffed and patted her own ass. "I like it just fine. See you at seven?" she asked.

Cole quirked an eyebrow. "Six works better for me. More time that way."

"Why not? I'm on vacation, right?" she said with a cock of her head, then turned on her heel and walked out the door. She made it as far as the car before allowing herself to feel how much her legs were shaking. *Shut it down. He's nothing special. Just some well-intentioned mountain-man Greek god or something. You got this.*

Those freakin' lips, though. So soft but commanding all at the same time. "Man, it has been too long," she said out loud. She pulled out of the drive onto the gravel road and felt her stomach flip at the thought of a date. Marie replayed the conversation and realized she hadn't pressed for specifics as to whether they were eating at his house or a restaurant. She wasn't going to lie to herself. She'd gone without sex for months. Marie wanted to go to Cole's house.

"I'll never see him again. Why not let my hair down?"

she rationalized as she craned her head around noticing she'd missed her turn and was driving by a big pen of donkeys. She threw the car in reverse and backed up, rolling down the window. *Actual donkeys.* She listened to them bray in her direction and made a mental note to drive around before she left to see what other unusual things she'd discover before returning to St. Louis. *Country people,* she thought with a smile.

Flipping through the clothes hung in the cabin closet, Marie decided to go with a soft gray sweater that offset her blue eyes perfectly. David used to tell her, when she wore it, her eyes were patches of blue sky peeping out over the clouds. Marie smiled at the memory then shuddered and pulled the sweater back over her head. Instead, she grabbed a different one, a red v-neck. She didn't want David haunting her tonight. She paired it with jeans, high-heeled booties, and flashy faux diamond earrings. She putzed around with her hair and decided to let the glossy, nearly black curls just do their thing.

Marie paced around the cabin and decided a shot of bourbon might help with her nerves. She poured two fingers in a glass and downed it, exhaling as the liquid burned her throat. A knock at her door jerked her out of her nervous internal monologue. "Here we go," she said to the ceiling and walked to the door.

She glanced through the peephole and mouthed a silent curse as she opened the door to Cole. He filled up the door frame, and the wicked smile on his face was enough to raise her temperature at least five degrees.

"Hello, Cole. Come on in," she said, side stepping against the door out of the way. Instead of walking around and ahead of her, he entered a few steps and turned, crowding her against the door.

"Marie," he said, arching an eyebrow. He dipped his head and pressed his lips to hers as his hand snaked its way gently to the nape of her neck, tipping her head back slightly with the lightest of pressure from his thumb on her jawline. It lasted only a few seconds, but she could feel that kiss down to the tips of her toes.

Marie was no stranger to kisses. She and Jesse teased frequently that up until David, there had been a veritable parade of men at Marie's disposal. She was smart, successful, and "sexy as all-get-out," in Jesse's words. And, to make it even better, she didn't "do" attachment. Marie was the poster child for picking up a hot man at a conference or vacation, doing some recon to determine he wasn't married, then enjoying herself.

She looked into Cole's eyes and felt a tiny shiver of anticipation dance down her spine. Instead of a little anxious, which was often her typical MO on actual first dates, Marie felt empowered. She braced herself against the door and felt her body's natural posture shift from neutral to chest and butt out, ready for fight or flight, or at least a really good roll in the hay.

Her hand found his in her hair, and she trailed her hand up his arm to his shoulder as the other crept up his side. She pressed against him and took his kiss, letting the feel-goods whirl throughout her body all the way down to her feet. She tried to recount if she'd ever been with a man his size. She was used to feeling petite, but she felt like a freakin' fairy next to him. Jesse had always teased and called her a wood sprite. Maybe she was right. She certainly didn't feel of this world with that man tasting her.

Cole lifted his head and straightened to his full height as he looked down his nose at Marie with a straight expression on his face. "Nope, didn't feel a thing. You?"

Marie laughed and slapped his arm. "Come on, Caveman. Where are you taking me?"

"Caveman?" he asked with a bemused expression.

"Yeah," she said, placing a hand on her sassy hip while he mulled over her choice of nickname.

"It fits. I like it," he said, swatting her on her behind as she stepped ahead of him. She turned to glare at him, but his playful expression made her smile instead.

This is a vacation. I don't have to be myself. I don't have to be pissed off all the time, she reminded herself as she followed him to his truck. She was going to have a wild time with this good-looking giant and go back to reality soon enough.

Cole opened her door and shut it once she was in the cab of his truck. "I believe you asked a question that I didn't answer. Are you okay with dinner at my place?"

Marie patted her stomach. "Sounds good to me. I'm starving!"

He smiled as he drove, appreciating a woman who would actually admit to enjoying food. For a moment, he let his mind linger on a memory a few years earlier of a night much like this. Jesse rarely entered his thoughts these days. He liked that she found her happy place with her new husband and family. It bothered him that there was distance between him and Levi now, but that was only natural. Cole pushed Jesse's memory back into the recesses of his mind. He didn't want any ghosts lurking about tonight. He'd been out on several dates since that night, but nobody had held his attention like the little firecracker sitting next to him. Marie seemed like a bomb that needed to be defused—carefully. Lucky for her, he had bucketloads of experience with just that from his service in the Marines. Cole wondered what she'd be like if she ever let her guard down fully. He loved a challenge.

In no time, they pulled up to Cole's home. "I think I said this the other day, but your place is gorgeous. Do you work nearby, or do you have a commute?" she asked, slipping out of his truck before Cole could circle around to open her door.

He stepped to the side so she could walk ahead of him to the door. "Most of the time I'm in the Shawnee. Works out well." He shrugged.

"Shawnee?" she asked as she turned in a circle, fully taking in the place.

He gestured all around. "The Shawnee National Forest." She shrugged. "Hmm, that's convenient. My drive is around half an hour when I'm in the office. The rest of my time is spent in airports and Ubers."

Cole's stomach turned at the idea of such a tiny woman stepping into a vehicle with a driver she didn't know. "What kind of work are you in?" he asked, unlocking the door and standing aside so Marie could walk in.

"Software sales. Fascinating stuff," she said, rolling her eyes. Cole took her coat and purse and settled them on a side chair in his living room. "Look at that view. Stunning!" she said, peering out over the woods. The sun had begun to set, and there were glimmers of light setting the woods off with pink, orange, purple, and blue hues.

Cole pulled a face and shivered. "I could never work at a desk," he said, stepping into the kitchen to wash his hands. "I need fresh air and trees, daily. Hey, steak and potatoes still sound good?"

"Sounds great. The food, not the work environment. I don't really do nature, bugs, or even mild discomfort." She grinned. "What can I do?" she asked, joining him at the sink.

"I've already got the grill warming up and the potatoes are baking in the oven. The salad is chilling in the fridge. What would you like with dinner? Want to open up a Cabernet?"

"I'm not much of a wine drinker. Do you have any bourbon?"

Cole's eyes lit up. "A woman after my own heart. How would a glass of Pappy Van Winkle do ya?"

"That'll do me just fine," she said with a bright smile.

"Here you go," he said, handing her a fresh bottle and two glasses. "You pour, I'll get the food on the grill. There are ice balls in the freezer if you take yours with ice."

Marie nodded. She fished around in the freezer until she found the ice balls, popped two to put in their glasses, and poured a healthy amount into each glass. Next, she put herself to work setting the table. By the time Cole came back in rubbing his hands on his arms from the cold, she'd finished and hopped up on the counter.

"Found the music, huh?"

"Yeah, do you mind?" she asked, hoping she'd picked a good selection.

"Can't go wrong with Alabama Shakes," he said quietly as he nestled himself between her knees from her perch on the countertop. He leaned in for a kiss, and after a minute, a smile spread to Marie's lips.

"What are you grinning at?" he asked as he moved his mouth to her neck. Goosebumps covered her skin as the tip of his tongue found the shell of her ear.

"I was just thinking that we're more than officially grown ups, and we've already spent most of our time tonight kissing."

"Kind of fun, though, isn't it?" he asked, pulling his head back to look into her eyes.

She nodded. "It is. I suppose there's not an *official* rule that we have to talk about the weather, politics, or the stock market."

"Wait, I can do both. It's colder than a witch's tit outside.

I'm a middle-of-the-roader and try to apply common sense when voting rather than party loyalty. What was the last one?" he asked.

"Stock market," she said, taking a sip from her drink.

"Ah. I'm glad I'm diversified," he said with a nod.

"Nicely done. I'll take your lips again now," Marie said, pulling him close.

Cole exhaled and quirked a brow at her as he pulled her closer to the edge of the counter. She could feel his arousal, clearly defined and pressed against her center. For ten cents she'd forfeit dinner and make a meal out of the man with the incredible arms. Their kissing intensified, and Cole's hands began to rove. When thoughts resurfaced, all Marie could think of was to pray that a timer wouldn't go off for the food.

Marie yelped in surprise when Cole settled his hands beneath her and lifted her from the counter. He walked her to the nearest wall and held her there like she was made of air.

Her legs instinctively wrapped around him, and a groan escaped her as he gently moved his hips against her. Rational thought was momentarily suspended as she let herself thoroughly enjoy every sensation Cole was stirring within her. She'd always fantasized about being picked up like this—just like in the movies—but it was an actual first. She suddenly praised instead of lamented every top-shelf item she couldn't reach, every dress that swam around her feet instead of fitting her petite frame, and every pair of cute jeans she'd ever had hemmed. It was worth it to feel light as a feather in this moment, as if she could be completely consumed by this giant of a man.

One of Cole's hands inched beneath the hem of her sweater, and Marie threw her head back and shouted, "Finally!"

His deep laugh fanned his breath against her skin. Her body responded as expected, and Cole made sure attention was paid with fingers and lips. Marie was ready to jerk her sweater over her head when the oven alarm started to beep.

Cole sighed and pressed his forehead against hers. "That's the alarm for the danged potatoes."

"Danged potatoes, is right," she said. "Put me down, Caveman. You're going to need your strength."

He threw his head back with a groan and a laugh, and let her down gently. "I'll never say I was glad you slid into that ditch… but…"

"But is right," Marie said. "Come on. Feed me."

DINNER WAS EXCEPTIONAL. Marie washed dishes and questioned her luck as Cole dried. Who runs into a ditch and meets a cooking, cleaning, sex god? Okay, so she couldn't quite call him a sex god yet, but if his make-out skills were any indication, she may have met her match.

"What's running through that head of yours?" Cole asked, startling her from her thoughts.

Marie looked him dead in the eye, feigning her most light-hearted voice. "Oh, just thinking about how good dinner was, and wondering if you're any good in bed."

Cole's eyes shifted from amusement to a building storm in a flash. He reached across her to turn off the faucet and took Marie's hands in his before toweling them off slowly. Marie's senses took in everything around her in that moment. "Lochloosa" by JJ Grey and Mofro played on the radio, slow and sultry. Their faces were reflected in the kitchen window over the sink. Light danced in the dark living room from the fireplace in the corner of her eye. Cole loomed beside her, pupils dark, head at a cocky angle.

A sly grin spread over his face as he leaned closer. "Now, let's see if I can curl those toes of yours," he said in a low voice next to her ear. A full-body shiver made Marie think he might just be able to do it.

"You're on," she answered.

"I like my odds. Come with me." He took her hand and led her back to his bedroom.

She paused long enough to grab her purse and Cole gave her a questioning look. "Protection... don't leave home without it."

He gave her a wicked grin. "I've got us covered." He started to take the purse from her hand and paused. "On second thought, we might need extra."

Her laugh bubbled up as she switched her focus to the feel of her hand in his as they walked through the hallway. The room was pretty minimal, but the furnishings were sleek. Cole led her to the bed and turned her so that she faced away from it. He placed his hand on the back of her neck and tipped her head back with a kiss. Using the slightest pressure, he eased her to a sitting position and only broke the kiss when he lowered himself to kneel before her.

Marie felt her heart rate pick up as he lifted her foot in his hands. He slowly unzipped her boot and pulled it from her foot before repeating the action. Cole held both hands upturned to her and tugged her gently with his fingertips when she placed hers in his. As she stood, he maintained his position on the floor and placed his hands at her ankles.

Her breath sounded shaky to her own ears as Cole encircled her ankles with his hands before he moved them up to her calves, where he paused for a squeeze. A few inches up, he squeezed at the back of her knees. His thumbs moved to the front of her legs as he worked his way up to the top of her thighs. Green-blue eyes met hers as he traced lazy circles on the way to the button and zipper of her jeans.

Before he finished unfastening her jeans, Marie had her sweater up over her head. She watched how his pulse ticked at the hollow beneath his jaw, and she couldn't wait to taste that spot. Cole rose as she began to lower herself, and his low, husky laugh tickled her ears as he braced his hands under her forearms to draw her up.

His lips found hers as Marie's hands traced the outline of his shoulders before they dipped lower over his chest and lower still. Cole groaned as she toyed with the hem of his shirt. He fisted a hand behind his neck and pulled the shirt from his body. Marie didn't lose any time touching his velvety skin.

Cole partially encircled her waist before his hands dipped under her ass. He hauled her up against him as she made a noise of surprise.

"Put me down," she squealed as she grabbed his shoulders frantically.

Cole laughed and pulled her closer. "What? Think I'm going to drop you?"

The stupidity of her concern registered as he easily adjusted her weight in his hands and rubbed her lace-covered center against his jeans-clad length. A moan left Marie's lips right before Cole took them with his own.

"Caveman," she whispered before sampling the spot her tongue had begged to taste.

COLE ROLLED TO his side and curled in behind Marie's sleeping form. He couldn't get over how tiny she felt in his arms. He'd always had a thing for tall women, but there was something about this feisty little mama that garnered his full attention. He felt her breathing shift and knew she was awake.

Slowly, Marie rolled over, a small smile on her face.

"Your hair is tickling my nose," he said, pulling his head back.

"Your breath is tickling my head," she answered testily, scrunching her face.

"Uh oh, not a morning person, huh?"

She moaned and threw a hand over her eyes. "Not even a little bit."

Cole sighed. "No chance of morning sex, then, huh?"

"No way. My breath could kill an elephant."

He bugged out his eyes and shimmied out of the bed. "Okay, I'll take the cue and go make some coffee. How do you take it?"

"Black, like my soul," Marie answered with a groan, listening for his reaction. She wasn't disappointed to hear his deep laugh resonate in the hallway.

After she finger-brushed her teeth and swept her hair into the ponytail holder she always kept handy, she dressed and went into the kitchen.

Marie hopped onto a barstool and watched Cole fish around in the refrigerator for breakfast goodies. "I didn't plan on staying over."

He surfaced with eggs and veggies for what she presumed would become an omelet.

"In your defense, you were a boneless heap of gratitude and too deeply exhausted to withstand the long journey home," he said with no small amount of smugness.

"Long journey, my foot," she answered, swatting him as she sidled up beside him to help dice the veggies.

"That's the part of the statement you took issue with? I don't know you as well as I thought," he scoffed.

"You don't know me at all," she answered, taking a big gulp of her coffee. She smiled when she said it, but Cole heard the undertone.

He pulled her into a hug and felt her stiffen for a second. Cole could've let go, but instead he held her gently and sighed. The way she relaxed into him reminded Cole of how a cat responds once it decides it doesn't hate you. They're all prickly at first, until they flop over and let you rub their belly. She was definitely prickly, but she was funny, too. *I want to know more*, he said to himself as he lightly scratched her back. Marie rested her head against his chest, and for a minute they were still together.

She felt tears gather in her eyes at the intimacy. *Get a grip, Marie*, she scolded. She raised her head back and smiled at Cole. He was attentive, she'd give him that. "Let's get to cooking. I'm famished."

Cole grinned. "If you liked my steak, wait till you try my omelets. They're my speciality.

"Your speciality, huh? I thought I'd already figured that one out last night," she teased.

"Drink your coffee, flirt," he said as he shooed her back to her seat. "Do you have plans for today?"

Alarm bells went off in Marie's mind. This was supposed to be a one-and-done thing. Honestly, though, she didn't have anything to do. She had only planned as far as a super awkward drive back to her cabin where she would take a bubble bath and replay the fascinating events of last night. She halfway wanted to stick to the plan and halfway wondered what the alternative would be. After another sip of coffee, curiosity got the better of her. "Well, I had planned on a bubble bath and a nap. How about you?"

"I was thinking about going on a hike. Want to go?" he asked as he sat an awesome-looking dish in front of her.

"In *this* weather?" she asked with huge eyes and a thumb jerked in the direction of the wall of windows reflecting a lightly snow-covered hillside.

"Yeah." He shrugged. "We would bundle up. It would be gorgeous out on Camel Rock."

Marie hitched her foot up on the counter and wiggled her toes in Cole's direction. "No way I'm hiking in heels. In case you hadn't noticed, my footwear is more fashion than function."

"Good point," he said around a mouthful of eggs. "Wait. What size shoe do you wear?"

Marie wrinkled her nose in distaste. "What, do you already have a creepy stalker pair of boots for me in your closet or something?"

"Eh, no… but Ryan's wife isn't much bigger than you. Maybe they have something that'll fit."

Marie mulled it over. "Maybe. Size seven."

"Do you have a warm coat?" he asked.

"I have the coat I wore when you picked me up on the road."

"Nope. That won't cut it. You eat, I'll see what I can rustle up," he said, placing his dish in the sink and whipping out his phone to call Ryan.

Marie listened to him talk as he gathered his things, presuming he was heading to the shower. She turned just in time to see a very naked Cole walk across the doorway into the bathroom. She couldn't decide which part of him was more beautiful: the muscled arms with the tattoo from his time in the Marines; the strong chest with the eerie wolf tattoo that he had explained is a symbol of loyalty and perseverance; or maybe her favorite part, his long, strong legs.

She had a definite thing for tattoos. Her favorite was discovering them on people she'd never dream had ink. It afforded an insight into their most private personality. She kept her own covered almost always. It was her own little secret. A little lotus flower snaked across her wrist, covered by her watch band. Her pink flower reminded her of how something beautiful can evolve from murky beginnings. It was funny how symbols could serve as sources of power.

While Cole was in the shower, she washed her face and finger-combed her hair into a semblance of normal, rather than a ratty, ponytail. Within just a few minutes she heard the water kick off. She milled around his living room lighting on what she was hoping to find—photos on another bookshelf.

A sepia-toned photo of a diapered boy, presumably Cole, sat on a smiling older man's lap. A girl in pigtails stood to the side of the chair, grinning from ear to ear. She found another of an unmistakable Cole in high school. He was more lightly muscled then, but still a sizable guy. He wore light denim jeans and a Big Johnson's t-shirt, huddled together with a group of guys all smiling with the carefree ignorance of youth. There was a high school football team photo, and then another photo from what she'd guess was a few years ago with Cole and a woman who looked like his twin. Her eye was drawn to a corner of a photo peeking out between two books. With a quick glance to be sure Cole was still in the bathroom, Marie gave in to her urge to snoop. Carefully, she pulled out a wrinkled photo of Cole during his service in the Marines. She took in how young he looked with his hair cut close. High and tight, she thought the style was called. Cole looked so young, smiling broadly in his dress blues with his arm wrapped around a stunning young woman. Marie squinted her eyes and noticed a diamond ring on the woman's left hand. Her mind swam with questions, and she jumped like she'd been shot when he opened the door and appeared in the hallway. Quickly she slid the photo back into place.

"So, I heard back from Ryan," he said.

"Well? Am I going out to freeze to death today?"

Cole grinned. "Looks like it. Seriously, though, I'll be sure you're dressed appropriately, and safe and sound. Ready for this?"

"I think so," she said warily. "You do remember that I don't *do* nature, right?"

"Give me one chance," he said, pulling her into an embrace. He lifted her hand to his lips. "Please?"

"If you aren't the biggest Prince Charming I've ever seen," she murmured. "Fine. I'll try anything once."

Cole leaned down and looked her in the eye with a mock hopeful look. "Really?"

"No. But, I'll go on a stupid hike with you," she answered with a fake sneer.

"Okay. Load up and we'll go get the gear from Ryan's."

Marie walked over to the couch and grabbed her purse. "Ready to roll."

Cole walked Marie to the passenger side of his truck and opened the door.

"Do you always do this?" she asked with a gesture toward the door.

"Where you're concerned, yes," he answered. "And don't go getting all ticked off with me over it. I was raised in the South where we were trained to have manners. It's not an insult, Marie. I know you're capable of opening your door. I want to do it for you. I like you. Will you let me?"

She sighed as she hoisted herself up into the cab of the truck. He truly seemed to mean it. "Yes," she said. "It's just different than anything I've experienced."

"That's fair," he said. "Can't all be gems like me, can they?" he asked with a wink.

Doesn't seem like it, Marie said to herself.

Suited up in proper hiking boots and the world's warmest down jacket, Marie tried her best to keep an open mind as she followed behind Cole. He was making the first set of tracks up the path, and she was trying to step where he stepped to avoid sinking into the snow. She couldn't help but grin at the number of times he turned back to check on her.

"Doin' alright back there?" he asked, stopping to pull down the sides of her hat to better cover her ears.

"Yeah, but if it wasn't for that accent of yours, there'd be no way I'd have agreed to this," Marie answered.

"Ah, a fan of the ole Tennessee accent? Well thank you kindly, ma'am," Cole said in an exaggerated tone as he dipped his head and pressed a kiss to her neck.

"Good Lord," Marie groaned. "Keep walking, soldier. There's apparently something worth trekking out in the snow to see."

Cole frowned down at her and looked arrogantly down his nose as his shoulders stiffened to his full height. "Soldier, huh?" he asked, crowding her a little. Marie edged back as Cole inched closer, resting his hands on her waist when she yelped as a wall of stone met her back. His lips melted into a wicked grin and he whispered, "Marines don't take kindly to being called 'soldier.'" His lips dipped down to claim hers, and Marie felt a swarm of butterflies flutter in her belly. "Anyway, military is right. How'd you know?" He pulled his head away and continued walking the path.

"Well, I saw…" Marie paused, realizing she would be confessing to snooping if she admitted she'd seen the picture he'd hidden of himself in his Blues with the woman.

He turned to look at her, encouraging her to keep talking. "I saw the Semper Fi tattoo, so that was a pretty good clue," she said in a teasing voice.

"Right. Very observant." He grinned. "Guess that one was hard to miss."

Marie blushed. His tattoo was over his heart, a place she'd been intimately acquainted with as he'd screwed her senseless.

"How long were you in?" she asked, desperate to will the flush from her cheeks as she cursed her pale complexion.

"Separated after the standard four years. I came close to re-enlisting, but I was ready to get into the woods. Bomb defusing doesn't hold a candle to working in forestry," he said in a flat voice.

"Bomb defusing?" Marie shrieked.

Cole gave a low chuckle at her visible shock. "EOD— Explosive Ordnance Disposal."

"Unreal," she said. Marie circled around him, took his hands in hers, and gave them a squeeze. Cole was puzzled by her sudden display of emotion.

She shook it off and gave him a little tug so they'd begin walking again. "I had a cousin that was an EOD soldier in Afghanistan. Scares the hell out of me to even think about that kind of pressure. You must either have nerves of steel or be crazy to do that job, right?"

He didn't miss the verb tense she used about her cousin. "Something like that," he answered. Cole stopped and pulled her in for a quick hug. "I'm sorry about your cousin."

When she pulled away, he let her. "Here, get behind me. It gets pretty narrow here."

"How much further?" she whined.

"Not much. It'll be worth it." Cole led the way up the narrow path and then stepped aside. They were standing on an outcropping of rocks. In the distance, set off by the morning sunlight, was the outline of a camel-shaped rock.

"That's beautiful!" Marie said with a smile. "I've never seen anything like this."

Cole watched her face as she took in the Shawnee National Forest. "You should see it in the fall when the trees are turning. It's amazing. There are some incredible waterfalls to see this time of year nearby. If you'd like to see them, I'd like to take you."

Marie nodded. "I think I'd like that. I can't believe I just said that."

He laughed and draped an arm around her shoulders. "Stick with me, and you'll try all kinds of new things."

She rolled her eyes in return, but the suggestion made Marie's pulse race. The walk back to the truck was quieter. Marie watched appreciatively as Cole moved ahead of her along the trail and thought about what she'd learned so far. He was massive. Undeniably sexy. The accent was to die for, and the manners far surpassed any of the men she'd been with... for whatever little time that had been. Marie mentally compared and contrasted Cole to David. The thought was so funny she snorted out loud as they reached the parking lot.

"What's that about?" Cole asked, brow quirked in confusion.

Marie shook her head and covered her mouth with her hand, willing herself to knock it off.

"Come on, tell me," he said as he held her door open.

She hopped up into the truck seat and turned her body to face him. "Just comparing you to the man I dated awhile back."

Cole stepped closer and nudged her legs apart so that he was inches away from her body. He looked down his nose at her with a challenging expression. "Well? How do I stack up?"

"Quite well, sir. Quite well. I mean, I know this is just a..." she gestured, fanning her hands back and forth, "just a fling, but whew! You make him look bad."

Cole grinned and reached his hands around to cup her butt. He pulled her body next to his until the only distance between them was the fluff of their down coats. "Good to hear, Marie. I'd hate to have to track him down and beat his ass."

Marie outright guffawed at that idea. David would have topped out at Cole's jaw. "While that's a tempting idea, it's not necessary," she said as she got herself under control. "He's out of the picture anyway. Currently occupied with a blonde Amazon goddess."

Cole nodded and stepped back as she swung her legs forward and buckled up. He shut the door and made his way around the truck. "How do you feel about that?" he asked as he entered the cab.

"About what?"

"How do you feel about your ex and the blonde Amazon goddess?"

She shrugged a shoulder. "Honestly, I'm fine with it. I mean, he can eat poop and die, but I have no issue with the goddess."

It was Cole's turn to laugh as he backed out of the parking spot. He placed his hand over the back of the seat as he drove and remembered how Marie had flinched the night they had met. He wanted to know if her ex was the reason she flinched.

"Were you together long?" he asked, keeping his voice neutral as the ugly thought of anyone hitting this amazing woman churned in his gut.

Marie felt immediately uncomfortable discussing David with Cole. She hadn't meant to bring up her flop of a relationship with someone she had no intention of seeing again once her little vacation in the woods was over. "For about a year." Her mind raced as she tried to think of a new subject to discuss. Donkeys. "So, the other day I missed your road and saw a huge group—a herd?—of donkeys. I don't think I've ever seen one in real life before. Weird."

Cole noted her subject change and decided not to press. "That would be the Barger Farm. Were you formally introduced to Wilbur?"

Marie narrowed her eyes at him. "What are you talking about?"

"I'll show you," he promised. "If you were out this way, you probably saw the peony farm, right?"

She furrowed her brow in confusion. "I don't think so. There's a flower farm here?"

"Yeah, it's really something. The family that owns it grow the prettiest flowers I've ever seen. They ship them all over to people, even send some up your way for the big farmer's market in the city. I've never been there, but I've heard it's something to see."

"Wow, who'd think something like that would be tucked away here," she said as she looked out the window.

Cole turned to her with a grin. "It's a pretty great little part of the world. All kinds of little treasures are tucked into these hills." Marie couldn't help but smile back. It was nice to see someone take pride in where they're from. So often it seemed like people would rather gripe than appreciate their hometown.

"Look to the right. Up on the hill, there. The fields are settled right in front of their house up there. It's something to see in late spring when they're in bloom."

Marie saw a gorgeous farmhouse backed by a large barn and acres of bare land. She could imagine what those acres would look like with bright pink pockets of peonies dotting the landscape. "I bet it's breathtaking!"

"There's usually a big crowd around Mother's Day with folks trying to get pretty pictures. There's a sunflower field a few miles out of town that people flock to also."

"An actual sunflower field?" she asked, eyes bright at the idea.

"Absolutely full of 'em. It's really pretty."

She nodded. "The owner must really love sunflowers. That's romantic."

Cole chuckled quietly. "Well, he loves dove meat."

Marie's head whipped around. "Dove meat?"

"Yeah, he plants the field so that the doves are attracted there during hunting season."

"Well that ruins the romantic slant, doesn't it?" she grumbled as he crooked a grin.

Cole drove until he eventually came upon the pen alongside the gravel road. Cole fished around in his glove box for something.

"What have you got?" she asked as he fiddled with a wrapper.

"You'll see," he said, throwing the truck door open.

Marie was instantly assaulted by the loudest braying sound she'd ever heard. One of the donkeys was going ballistic as they approached the pen.

"Is something wrong with it?" Marie asked, half-hidden behind Cole. "Hey, what are you doing?" she asked as he stuck something in her coat pocket.

"Wait and see. And no, nothing's wrong with him, Wilbur's just happy to have company. Cole threw his hand up toward the farmhouse where a little blonde woman had stepped out on the porch to see what the fuss was all about. She waved back to Cole and stopped abruptly to cuss an Australian Shepherd dog that had ripped her dish towel out of her hands and took off across the snowy yard. The woman gave up, shook her head, and went back inside.

"Marie, Wilbur. Wilbur, Marie," Cole said, making a showy gesture of planting a smooch on the donkey's nose.

"I cannot believe you just did that," she said in abject horror.

"I know. Kinda gross, but he loves smooches almost as much as he likes peppermints." Cole grinned. He stepped into the gated pen and held the door out for Marie. Reluctantly, she followed.

"Peppermints? How does one find out that donkeys like… AH! Son of a bitch! I think it's trying to bite me!" she shrieked and ran for the gate.

"Come back!" Cole laughed. "He won't bite, I promise. Get over here. You can impress your city friends with tales of how us goofy bastards amuse ourselves here in the country."

Marie tried to get her eyes back in their sockets as she walked over to Cole, who was petting Wilbur.

"Here, turn to the side and hold your pocket out," he suggested.

She did, and couldn't help but get tickled when Wilbur snuffled around until he found her pocket. With his lips he picked out the soft peppermint that Cole had unwrapped and stuck in her coat.

"Yeah, nobody's going to believe this unless there are pictures," she mused.

"Here then, we can fix that," Cole said, whipping out his phone. He stretched out his arm and took a picture of the three of them: Marie, Cole, and a minty-breathed Wilbur.

Something warm tugged at Marie's heart at the gesture.

He was a hook-up. She didn't take selfies with hook-ups. They walked back to his truck, and Marie helped herself to a heaping dose of hand sanitizer from her purse. Cole's blue-green eyes twinkled with amusement as she inspected her coat pocket.

"There's donkey snot on Amy's coat now," she said, her face twisted in disgust.

"Trust me, she's married to Ryan. Gross is her love language," he said with a smile.

Cole pulled up to her cabin and frowned as Marie hopped out of her side of the truck. She caught his look and threw her hands up in the air. "Sue me! It's a hard habit to break!" He caught her off guard with his big laugh.

"What am I going to do with you?" he asked, holding his hands out for the key to her cabin to unlock the door for her."

"No idea, but I look forward to finding out," she flirted. Cole just shook his head and waited outside the threshold.

"I'm running into town to grab some groceries. Can I get you anything?"

"Nah, I'm planning on getting out tomorrow. I think I'll hole up for the rest of the day and relax," she said.

"Sounds good to me." Cole pulled Marie into a hug and leaned down to place a warm, gentle kiss to her lips. "Talk to you soon."

"Bye," she answered. "Have a good day." Marie shut and locked the door behind her and walked into the kitchen. Tea, a hot bath, and a nap would do wonders right about now, she decided. *Stop smiling*, she told herself. *It's just sex.*

six

MARIE DROVE THROUGH THE town and decided to try a cute little cafe she was sure she'd heard Jesse mention. She had placed her lunch order and was milling around the shop admiring the locally made goods. The bell over the door jingled continually as people came to shop and grab a quick bite. She moved to the back wall of the cafe to check the price on a set of dishes she was sure she couldn't live without when she felt a strange sensation. A tingle started low in her spine and thrummed its way to her neck. The atmosphere was charged, like a lightning bolt was about to hit. As Marie turned her head, a fingertip traced a line from her neck down her back, and a shudder rippled through her. Cole stared down with a smug grin, and Marie felt the heat rise to her cheeks.

"Didn't expect to see you here," she said, noticing how most of the clientele was yoga-pants-wearing mothers and grandmothers clucking over adorable children.

Cole grinned and pressed a quick kiss to her neck. "What do you mean? I'm in touch with my feminine side. I love a good chicken salad croissant."

A small laugh escaped her. Marie heard another giggle and turned to catch the stare of the woman behind the counter. Cole looked over and nodded his head in greeting to the tiny little blonde. Her platinum hair was cut in a sexy pixie cut with long bangs, and a tiny tattoo graced her wrist. She looked like she'd be more at home performing at a rock concert than serving lunch in a fancy cafe. A spark of jealousy ignited in Marie. Who was she to Cole? Former flame? Current? Marie tamped down that feeling and reminded herself that he was just a distraction anyway. Why would she give two hoots if he had a thing with the waitress.

"Want your usual, Cole?" the woman called over, her lips set in a sultry smile. Marie stifled a laugh.

He wrapped his arm around Marie casually and answered, "Yes, ma'am, that would be great."

Marie didn't miss the flinch on the goddess's face. *"Easy there, lady. I'll be gone in a few weeks,"* she muttered.

"What's that?" Cole asked with a smile.

"Nothing, just mumbling." Marie stepped out from under his arm as she checked the price on a tumbler.

"Marie? Your order is ready."

The little blonde bombshell was at her elbow. "Cole, will you be joining her?"

"That alright with you?" he asked Marie.

"Of course." She smiled.

"Marie, this is Charlotte. She owns the cafe. Charlotte, Marie is renting one of Ryan's cabins for a while."

Charlotte extended a hand tipped in black lacquered nails. Marie felt a surge of 90s nostalgia.

"Nice to meet you. I love the polish."

"Thanks! All I need now are some Doc Martins and I'll be back in my happy place," Charlotte answered.

"Me, too. I still have the hair," Marie joked, cupping the curls that brushed the tops of her shoulders.

Charlotte smiled. "Your table is ready. I'll bring Cole's food over when it's up."

Cole placed his hand on the small of Marie's back, and they walked over to the seating area.

"Friend of yours, eh?" Marie asked with an arched brow.

He smiled in answer but didn't comment.

"Gentleman never tells, is that it?" she pushed.

Cole shrugged his shoulders. "What are you up to today?" He smiled politely at the waitress Charlotte had dispatched to deliver his lunch. "Thank you." He nodded.

Marie decided to accept his change of topic with what little grace she had left to muster. "Not much. Running a few errands in town, then heading back home."

Cole crooked a grin at her choice of words but knew better than to voice them. He'd figured out quickly that she was about as prickly as a woman could be. He couldn't help but wonder why she was so cautious one minute and sassy as hell the next. It's like she was in constant battle which aspect of her personality was dominant. *Part of the fun,* he thought. *Would be exhausting long-term, though.*

seven

A FEW DAYS LATER MARIE SHOOK her head in disbelief. "How did you talk me into this?" Marie asked Jesse, throwing a glance behind her. Thirty-five sleeping middle school band students certainly filled up a school bus in all capacities: seats, sounds, and smells. There was enough scented body spray in the air to choke a horse.

You would not believe the smell on this bus. I'm having total flashbacks - Marie

I'm shocked you went. - H.C.

Trust me, I can't believe it either. - Marie

She put her phone back in her pocket and wrinkled her nose at the cloud of hormones and perfumed air.

"Calm down, it's not that bad," Jesse said, hiding her

laugh behind her hand. "It's not as bad as it was on the ride here, right? At least they're quieter this time."

Marie feigned disgust and answered in a voice thick with sarcasm. "This is just how I wanted to spend my vacation. Surrounded by hormones."

"Walking, talking hormones is my specialty. Speaking of how you're spending your time—I haven't seen as much of you as I'd like. I'm glad you agreed to come on the band trip. The lock-ins fly by. Usually, though, I'm stuck talking to the other moms. Thankfully, you're a distraction." Jesse grimaced and cocked her head toward one of the other field trip sponsors.

Marie furrowed her brow. "What's the big deal with the other moms? They look nice enough."

"Oh yeah. They look nice enough. Don't let their matching boots and blow-outs fool you. They're vicious," Jesse replied as she curled her fingers into claws. "See that one with the Botox forehead?"

"Jeez, Jesse. Judgy much?" Marie exclaimed. "I had Botox injections for my wrinkles years ago," she said, pointing between her eyebrows.

"Yeah, but you weren't a bitch to me the other day. Let me finish." Jesse threw up her hands in surrender. "And okay, fine. That was rude. Anyway, the gal over there has asked me for the two years we've lived here which teacher I was requesting for my youngest. This year, in an effort to make conversation, I asked her. She acted aloof, said that she was going to pray about it and take what the Lord provided, but she'd be happy to ask around for me to find out who's a good teacher. First off, she didn't fool me for a minute. You know as well as I do she's got a teacher picked out and is keeping it top secret. And two, why in the actual hell would I want her to ask around for me?"

Marie stared blankly at her friend. "You need to get out more. Leave this place and come back to the city where you work in an office with actual people again."

Jesse sighed. "Clearly you are right. Some of this small-town stuff I did not actually miss. The bulk of it is pretty fantastic, though." Jesse looked out the bus window as they passed over the Ohio River. "Oh, did I tell you Mallory is all moved in?"

"Which one is that again?" Marie asked, replaying the names of everyone Jesse had mentioned on their hour-long drive as they caught up.

"This gets a little tangled, so hold on. Mallory is my cousin. She's Jake's sister."

"The cop, right?" Marie clarified.

"Well, he's a cop. Mallory is a nurse. She just moved back and is renting Avery's cabin."

Marie thought for a second. "And Avery's the doctor?"

"Yes. She's a psychiatrist, but that's not even the crazy part."

"Punny," Marie jabbed.

"Thank you," Jesse said with a laugh. "Anyway, Mallory moved back and is renting Avery's cabin since Avery is living with Jake now."

"Do you think they'll get married?" Marie asked, getting more interested in the gossip as they went.

"I do. They're both chicken when it comes to marriage, but they're in the process of adopting the sweet little boy they're fostering, and that might make the process go a little more smoothly. Fair or not, that's how it goes," she said with a shrug. Jesse continued, "Here's the crazy part. Mallory is seriously dating Avery's friend Cade."

"You said that weird. What's up with that arrangement?"

Jesse looked behind her to make sure a kid wasn't lurking nearby. "Avery and Cade used to be friends with benefits," she said with a waggle of her eyebrows.

"Jake's girlfriend? Whoa! How's he with all that?"

"Honestly, I think it grosses him out, but he's trying to play nice. It's impossible to be around Cade and not like him. Plus, it's not like Jake was an angel between the time he divorced that nut job and when he and Avery hooked up. He doesn't have much room to judge."

"Do you have pictures of these people? I think it would help me keep them straight. I feel like I need one of those people maps like you see on cop shows. The ones with the string going from point A to B to keep it all together," Marie said, pointing her finger at all the imaginary photos.

Jesse shrugged. "I know. It's convoluted. But the cool part is the family just seems to get bigger and bigger. I love that."

A pang of sadness hit Marie unexpectedly. Her family certainly wasn't getting any bigger anytime soon. She enjoyed hearing Jesse's crazy stories of her brood, and she sometimes felt disappointed that her life didn't work out that way.

"How's your mom doing?" Marie asked halfway to keep herself away from the sad thoughts and halfway out of genuine concern.

Jesse paused as she tried to find the right way to answer. "Overall, much better. I mean, the sadness doesn't go away just because the days go by. I don't think you can truly get over the death of your spouse. She and Dad were like two peas in a pod."

Marie patted Jesse's hand.

Jesse gave a small smile of thanks. "She's getting out more. I think it maybe helps a little that her sister Ruthie got married and isn't over so much. I don't mean that in a bad way," she quickly backtracked. "Ruthie was good medicine for Mom after Dad died, but it's easy to not look for ways to fill your time if it's automatically filled for you. Know what I mean?"

"I think so," Marie answered.

"She's gotten more involved with church functions over the past few months. We have a very active women's group at our church. They're either cooking for weddings or funerals, stuffing bears for the bear ministry, or putting together sack lunches for the free-lunch kiddos.

"Hold up. Bear ministry?" Marie asked in confusion.

"Yeah! They sew little stuffed bears that get handed out to kids at the hospital, and most of our officers keep a small bagful with them in case they go out on a call and have to take a child in their cruiser. It gives them a little something to focus on and snuggle during a scary time."

"Good grief," Marie said, wiping a tear from her eye. "That got me."

"I know. Gets me, too, when I think about it," Jesse agreed. She blew out a quick breath. "So, on the upside, she's got some really great ways to fill up her days. There's a fairly recent widower that keeps eyeballing her across the aisle at church. He asked her to lunch one day, and I swear I thought she was going to faint away dead on the spot."

Marie's eyes were wide. "Really? Church as a pick-up spot?"

"Hey, don't knock it until you try it. I had a guy hit on me at church once, and it was so hot I thought the place would catch on fire."

Marie chuckled at the imagery. "Or at least have the doors fall off the church, right?"

"Right," Jesse agreed. "God, that guy was a sexy beast but crazy as a bed bug.

"I don't remember this one. I thought the world began and ended with Levi?" Marie teased.

"Well, of course!" Jesse joked good naturedly. "But, even the sainted Levi lapsed into a moment of assholishness when he eh, *reconnected*, with an ex," she said quietly as a student passed by on their way to the snack stash at the front of the bus.

Marie wrinkled her un-Botoxed brow as she tried to access the information Jesse was talking about. That was a handful of years ago, and she'd slept since then. Something was forming, but she couldn't put her finger on it.

"I had some fun of my own during that little fiasco. An old high school friend started coming around and curling my toes from time to time. I still see him every now and then, but it's still weird, ya know? Once you get used to looking at a man from the eyes up, it's hard to envision him otherwise," Jesse said with a cackle.

Marie laughed. "Got wild, huh? How wild? Like, fake-yoga/real-sex-swing wild?"

Jesse snorted. "Seriously? I'd probably hang myself or get stuck and need the Jaws of Life to get me out. Can you imagine the bruising on my squishy thighs?" she said as she squeezed her curvy thighs.

"Oh stop! You look amazing," Marie said, swatting her friend on the leg. "So this guy is still around?"

Jesse nodded, taking a sip from her travel mug of coffee.

"Awkward. Does Levi know about it?" she asked, wondering how people who know everybody's business survive all the gossiping.

"It's a little uncomfortable. He and Cole used to be close, so basically he lost a friend over it," she said with a sad expression.

Marie's heart slammed in her chest. "Did you say…"

"Mom!" Jesse's son Ryan peeked over the seat and both women jumped guiltily.

Jesse was the first to unclench. "Good grief, you scared me. What's up?"

"Can you come back here and help me? I can't get my sleeping bag rolled up, and it's taking up too much room."

Jesse rolled her eyes at Marie and stood up. "Why in the heck would you unroll it on the bus, son?"

"It got cold, so I was trying to warm up and sleep," he said, in no way calculating the number of gross germs that were likely now on his sleeping bag like his mother was doing.

"Be right back," she said to Marie and made her way to the back of the bus.

Marie's head swam as she tried to remember details about Jesse and Cole. She put her head in her hands and rubbed at her temples, begging her logical brain to try and calculate the statistics of her having the best sex of her life with a guy her friend had had a fling with.

Jesse tapped Marie on the shoulder with a look of concern. "You okay?"

"Well… I don't know." She shifted in her seat so that Jesse could reclaim her seat. Her friend waited for clarification. "You said your toe-curler's name was Cole, right?"

Jesse nodded with a slight grin.

"Cole Green? Big dude? Good hair. Sexy eyes. Mysterious as all get out?"

Jesse's face went serious. "Yes. Why?"

Marie exhaled. "He's the reason I've been MIA since I got here."

"Noooooo!" Jesse said in utter shock. "Are you serious?"

Tightly, Marie nodded. "Yeah."

"What are the mother trucking odds?" Jesse said, leaning her head back against the seat.

"See? This is why we're friends. That's right where I went," Marie said, throwing her hands up in exasperation. "This makes me sick to my stomach. I mean, not because you're gross or anything. What?" she said with eyes as wide as saucers at Jesse's dirty look.

"I'm not gross!" Jesse exclaimed.

Marie waved her offense away. "That's what I said! What I mean is… I don't know. It's just gross."

Jesse nodded. "You're right. It's gross. And awkward."

Marie nodded again. "Well, crap. It figures. I mean, he's amazing."

Jesse shuddered. "It's true," she said with a nervous giggle.

Marie rubbed her hands down her face. "Unbelievable."

Jesse shrugged. "Well, what are you going to do. It happens."

"It doesn't happen in St. Louis," Marie said with mock horror.

"Sure it does. People probably just don't talk about it as openly. It's more about who went to high school where rather than who did you sleep with last week, right?" she said with a roll of her eyes. "Sleeping with someone a friend was with at some point is basically the small-town dating version of required reading for school. It's going to happen, so why fight it?"

"You're probably right," Marie admitted. "It was nice while it lasted."

"I don't mean to be tacky, but other than being slightly gross, why is this a show-stopper? You're only here for a little while longer, right?" At Marie's nod, she continued. "I remember someone getting in my face and reminding me that as long as I wasn't setting up false expectations, there was no reason to do anything other than enjoy myself."

Marie shrugged her shoulders. "I said that?"

"Yes. Ironically, it was about Cole," she said with a grimace.

"Jesus," Marie hissed.

"Hazard of a small-town sex life," she teased in return.

Marie mulled it over. "And you wouldn't have a problem with it?" she asked Jesse.

"I mean, it's weird as all hell, but honestly, it might be a way to bring Levi and Cole back to some sort of friendship," she said, waggling her fingers.

Marie watched Jesse as the wheels turned. Her friend thrived on chaos and large gatherings of people she loved. "You're going to use me as a buffer, aren't you?" she accused.

"Maybe. But I'd bet the farm that's not the only thing you're buffing," Jesse said with a poker face.

"Oh my God. Enough!" Marie said, waving her off.

Jesse shrugged, laughing at her own joke. "Get your crap gathered up, lady. We're at the school."

Marie was shocked to see the last leg of the trip had flown by. *Guess that's what happens when you find out you've been sharing a lover with one of your best friends,* she mused then shuddered. *It's not like we're dating,* Marie reminded herself.

eight

THE NEXT AFTERNOON COLE shuffled into Marie's kitchen, arms laden with grocery bags.

"What did you get?" she asked, peeking around his shoulder.

He laughed at the eager look on her face. "How do you feel about smoked salmon and veggies?" he asked.

"Are you a chef as well as a forester?" she teased.

"A man has his secrets," he said, looking down his nose at Marie as he passed her a bottle of wine from the grocery bag.

She'd been waiting for an opening, and it didn't get much better than that. "Speaking of secrets, I found out one of yours," Marie said as she opened the bottle.

"Yeah? What's that?" he asked, taking two glasses down from the shelf.

"You and Jesse had a thing, and you didn't mention it to me," she said, aiming for the casual tone she'd rehearsed. The guilty look on his face transformed her from casual to livid. "Ah! I see. I had thought maybe you were doing the white knight, I don't kiss and tell thing again, but I can see by your face you didn't think I'd find out. What the hell, Cole?" she said with a wince. She sounded like a nag even to her own ears.

Cole wasn't used to being talked to like an idiot. His own temper began to flare at her accusatory tone. "Wait a minute, Marie. Have I asked you for a list of people you've slept with prior to me? Why should I tell you that Jesse and I were together a few times?"

She glared at him in disbelief. "Are you kidding me right now? You should have told me because she's my friend! How awkward do you think it was for me to blurt out that we've been screwing around after she mentioned being with a guy named Cole before she and Levi were back together?" Marie screeched. As a heavy silence fell on the kitchen, Marie's phone rang.

She jerked it off the counter and answered with a brisk hello. Cole watched as the blood drained from her face as she spoke one-word answers into the phone. After ending the call, Marie shakily walked to the barstool and squinted at the phone as tears welled in her eyes.

"What?" Cole asked, hating that he even cared after just being scolded like a dog by her.

She placed the phone down on the counter and placed

her face in her hands. "My ex-husband. He's been released from prison."

Cole hid his surprise as she looked up to gauge his reaction. "Prison?"

She nodded. "He was there for manslaughter. He killed his next wife, the one after me." A shiver ran down her spine. She hated talking about Kevin and that portion of her life.

He slid into the seat next to Marie and waited for her to say something. "Want to talk about it?" For a second, she simply stared at nothing.

"Here," he said, standing and holding his hand out to hers. She took it, and he led her to her couch. He sat down and pulled her down on his lap, her head resting against his chest. She pissed him off to no end, but she fit him so well.

In a tumble of words, Marie told Cole about how Kevin hit his second wife, and that her murder was technically an accident because she'd fallen and hit her head. She explained how the charges were filed and how long he'd been there.

"Marie?" he asked. She looked up into his eyes. "Did he ever hit you?" A defiant look crossed into her eyes.

"Twice," she said, holding up two fingers. "I was stupid enough to stay after the first time, but not the second. He was an awful drunk. Really loud and angry. Kevin was lazy as all get out. The only time he would bother throwing any energy into anything was cashing his paycheck so that he could go drink it, or screaming at football games on TV. God, I can still see the beer cans littered all over our living room. I'd come home from work and find them everywhere.

He worked construction, so on rainy days, he'd get home before me and get a head start on getting smashed. We were poor as church mice at that time. I couldn't believe he'd waste what little money we had on booze."

Cole's heart raced at the thought of some asshole laying hands on a woman. Any woman, but especially Marie. She noticed the change in the set to his jaw. "You okay?" she asked, confused at his reaction.

She saw the muscle tic in his jaw before he spoke. "I can't stand men that terrorize women." His tone was so predatory that Marie flinched. "My dad used to hit my mom."

Marie's hand went to his chest. Cole covered it with his own, and he continued talking. "It was awful. I remember being a little kid and hearing the furniture get knocked around. I must've been about five, the first time I remember, anyway. Mom tried to be quiet, I guess, so that me and my sister wouldn't get scared. One time I remember we ran into the room, and she hollered in a weird voice for us to go to bed. I still remember my dad with his hand held in the air, his belt hanging from it. He turned back and smiled at me before laying into her with it. I grabbed my sister and we hid in the closet 'til it was quiet. I put Kelly to bed in my room with me. She's a little under a year younger than me. Irish twins, my mom called it."

"Cole, I'm so sorry."

He shrugged his shoulder. "It went on for years until I finally got big enough to knock him on his ass. I was in high school at that point. My dad was huge. He was either drunk or high on something; that's the only reason I think I was able to take him. While he was down, my mom grabbed her purse and we ran out with the clothes on our backs. We drove straight from Tennessee to here, where my grandparents lived. He never came for us. He was probably relieved we were gone."

"What's wrong with people," Marie asked quietly.

Cole folded his arms around her. "People have their reasons and their troubles," he said in a hushed voice. "It still never justifies hurting someone." He heaved a huge sigh and continued, his words a near-murmur into her hair, "Marie, I'm sorry I didn't tell you about Jesse. I was afraid you'd stop seeing me for what little time I have left with you."

She accepted his apology with a nod. As Cole held her close, Marie felt her anger with him subside. There wasn't any real harm done at this point if she was completely honest. Her inner control freak was just going to have to sit this one out. She had bigger concerns at the moment.

The next morning Marie and Cole were woken up by a text message from Jesse.

"Housewarming party for Mallory tonight at 6:00. We have to bring some good juju in to replace the bad juju left from the shooting. Bring Cole." - Jesse

"Did I read that right?" Marie asked as she squinted at the phone and held it for Cole to read.

"Yup. Looks like we're making this Facebook official," he said with a low laugh.

"Not that, *dummy*," she said with a roll of her eyes. "What is she talking about juju and a shooting?"

"Oh yeah," he said. "Hold on, this gets complicated without a diagram," Cole said in a low laugh. "That's how it is in small towns, though. You know the details on everybody."

Marie rolled her eyes. This was so not like life in St. Louis. In a city, you had your little circle and then the rest of the goings-on came from the news. Apparently this place had one ongoing saga after another, and everybody knew each other's business.

"So," he started, "Jesse's cousin, Jake, is a cop. He lives out in the boonies on Poets Pass, just down the road from Jesse and Levi, actually. Anyway, Jake fell for his neighbor, Avery. Avery's a shrink. Last year, she had a client go absolutely nuts. Certifiable. The whack job stalked her for months and eventually broke into her house. She shot him and started staying with Jake."

"My God! Did he die?" Marie asked in horror.

"Yeah," Cole said casually, then added, "but not right then. Avery didn't kill him, she just wounded him pretty bad. The guy died when he charged the hospital security guard and was shot. Talk about a media firestorm. They made us out to be a bunch of toothless hillbillies down here. I don't know why the people on the news can't pick someone who actually has all their teeth to interview when something goes down. The same thing happened when we had a horrible tornado a few years back. I can't believe you didn't hear about that one, even in St. Louis."

She shrugged. "We definitely heard about the tornado. How horrible."

He looked up, and she saw the heaviness of the memory in his eyes. "It was. So much destruction in such a small amount of time. It was something to see how our town pulled together after that. Our whole area, really. That's the good thing about places like this. There might be little sports rivalries here and there, even a little competition about which little town is better to live in, or be from... but in the end we all have one another's backs."

Marie nodded and wondered what it would be like to grow up in that kind of atmosphere. It seemed hard to fathom. "Regarding the shooting, though, we'd never hear about that one. Up there, shootings are a nearly every morning occurrence on the news. A person just gets used to it, I guess. But, seriously, someone was shot at the house, and Mallory decided to move there of all places?"

"Eh," he answered with a shrug. "From what I heard, she was an ER nurse in Chicago prior to moving here. Nothing much phases her, I bet. Plus, it's a really cool place from what I've seen on the outside. And her brother lives right next door, so that probably helps."

Marie just shook her head. "First question, how do you get the scoop on everything living at the top of *this* mountain?"

Cole grinned. "Remember Charlotte from the cafe? She

catches every bit of talk there is in this town. She could write a book on this place."

Marie shot him a dirty look. "Second question. While we're clearing the air—what's between you and Charlotte?"

Cole tilted his head in mild annoyance. "We went out a few times, but nothing serious. We've been friends for years. That was a long time ago."

Marie could accept that. "Next question, what is it with this place that makes all this drama not seem like a big deal?"

"What do you mean?" he asked, leaning on an elbow.

She echoed his pose. "It just seems like a lot of stuff goes on here, and nobody gets super flustered about it." Marie mentally played back Jesse's surprisingly unshaken response to finding out Marie had been sleeping with her previous lover.

"Sometimes," he said, rolling her to her back and placing her phone on the side table, "you just have to stop, take stock of what you have, figure out what you can control, and," he paused, nipping the spot at the top of her shoulder, "roll with the rest of it." He emphasized the word roll with a roll of his hips. Suddenly, Marie was less concerned with anything other than the man set on getting her full attention.

nine

Jesse's husband Levi was the first to greet Cole and Marie as they walked into Mallory's housewarming party. Marie took in Cole's tight smile as Levi greeted them in the driveway where he was unloading charcoal from the bed of his truck. "Cole, Marie, welcome. Help yourself to some food." He gestured toward the house.

"Levi, thanks for the invitation," Cole said. Marie watched with her heart in her throat during the moment Levi paused before shuffling the bag of charcoal to his other arm and grabbing Cole's arm in one of those manly clasp/hit-on-the-back exchanges.

"Good to see you, man. Jesse's got a margarita machine going at full blast in there, too. Beer, water, and sodas are in the coolers on the deck." That was about as far as they were going to get in manspeak.

"Sounds good, thanks," Cole answered. "Can I get you anything?" he asked as he turned to Marie.

"Go ahead, I'll be there in a sec," she answered with a smile. Once Cole was out of earshot, she spoke to Levi. "Thanks for including us."

"You bet. Keep your eye on that guy," he said with a tight smile. Marie had the feeling he was trying to be light-hearted, but the sentiment didn't carry.

Marie plastered a smile on her face and walked over to where Cole was filling a plate. "Anything look good?" she asked, trying not to laugh at the pile of wings on his plate.

He gave a boyish grin and leaned down to whisper in her ear. "Sorry, but there's a mean little woman that worked me to the bone today. I've got to get my energy up. Who knows what she's got in store for me later on."

She looked up to the sky, faking shock at his audacity. Jesse picked that moment to wrap Marie in a hug.

"Hey! You guys made it. I'm glad. Did you get drinks yet? Did you get a tour?" she fussed.

"Hey, Jesse. Nice to see you. Marie, beer?"

"Definitely. Stout, if they have it," she answered. Cole grinned at her choice. "I'll go grab a few." He nodded at Jesse as he took leave of the ladies.

Jesse blew out a breath. "Okay, that's over. I can act normal now."

"Normal…" Marie said with an exaggerated roll of her eyes.

"As normal as I get, that is," she said, pinching Marie on the arm. Come with me. I'll give you the grand tour."

"Including the chalk outline of the body?" Marie asked, feigning nonchalance.

"Don't be silly. He didn't die here. He just nearly bled to death," Jesse answered. She gave as good as she got.

"So, is Avery here?" Marie asked, looking around for an unfamiliar face.

"Nah, it's still a little weird for her to be here. She's a tough cookie, but that night did a number on her."

Marie nodded in understanding, wondering how she'd handle it if she had to do something so drastic to defend herself.

They made it as far as the master bedroom when they heard arguing on the other side of the door. With a quick exchange of glances they skittered quietly down the hall and made a big show of exclaiming over the newly laid hardwood floors to give whoever was arguing a little warning that there were ears around. The door opened, and Jesse jumped right in to introductions.

"Perfect timing! Mallory, Cade, this is Marie, my friend from St. Louis. She's renting a cabin from Ryan Drake out near Eagle Mountain."

"Nice to meet you," Mallory said. "Did you get any food yet? Smells amazing in the kitchen."

"Not yet, but that's my next stop after the tour," Marie replied.

"Nice to meet you," Cade answered tightly, then he

walked down the hallway. Jesse shot a look after him and glanced at Mallory.

"He's being an asshole," Mallory whispered. "He'll get over it."

"They always do," Jesse concurred.

A cheery voice bellowed from the kitchen. "Mallory? Where are the trash bags? You don't keep them under the sink like I do. Darned kids, they have to improve on everything," Ruthie said, yammering away at her husband, Hank, who stood smiling dutifully by her side.

Mallory turned to Marie and rolled her eyes. "Marie, make yourself at home. I'm going to show my mother, again, where I keep the trash bags." Mallory turned in the opposite direction of Cade, who by the look on his face, was headed straight for the beverages.

"Wonder what the argument was about," Jesse said in a quiet voice. She walked Marie through the room and whispered. "This is where Avery shot that bastard. She nailed him! I'll have to tell you that story. It's unreal. I was here that night and knew something was up, but I had no idea what. It was scary as all get out. I think Jake is going to drop by, but I'm not sure if he's here yet. I'll save that one for later. Don't want to get busted retelling it."

Marie nodded. "Think Mallory would mind if I use her bathroom?"

"Not a bit," Jesse said, gesturing to the door. "I'll be in here."

Marie walked a few steps into the bedroom and stepped

into the gorgeously appointed bathroom. Jesse had explained that they'd basically gutted the bedroom and bathroom. Avery wanted to keep the property since it was such a good spot of land, but she couldn't stomach just having the floors cleaned. Marie washed up and looked around to be sure everything was how it ought to be when she saw it.

"Jesse," she hissed. "Get in here!"

Jesse cautiously opened the door. "What's wrong?"

"I bet I found what they were arguing about." She pointed to the trash can where a pregnancy test box was clearly visible.

"Oh my gosh!" Jesse mouthed. She peered into the trash can. "I don't see the pee stick. I'm going in," she said, rolling up her sleeve.

"Don't you dare!" Marie said, pulling her friend away from the trash can. "Sometimes it's better not to know what you're not supposed to know!"

Jesse frowned. "Ugh! I hate the voice of reason."

"I know. I can be no fun sometimes," Marie agreed. "It'll be better this way. Plus, your poker face is crap."

"Man. It's the worst, isn't it?" Jesse asked, eyes wide.

Marie nodded in agreement. The pair circled around to the kitchen where Marie could grab a snack. Jesse peeked out the window and noticed Cole and Levi were gathered around a large bonfire, talking. She smiled smugly and turned to see Marie watching her.

"What are you smiling at?" Marie asked, taking a huge bite out of her sandwich.

"Oh, just congratulating myself on being a genius," she said with a smile.

Marie quirked a brow of confusion her way. Jesse pulled her over to the window.

"Look, they haven't spoken in a few years, and they're talking now like old frien—"

Jesse stopped talking when Marie's eyes went round in surprise. She turned back to the men and saw Levi throw a punch at Cole's jaw. Jesse ran for the door with Marie on her heels.

"You were my friend! I still can't believe you did that to me!" Levi yelled as Cole got right in his face.

"What did you think? That you owned her? That you had some kind of dibs or something because of what happened years and years ago? That's screwed up, man!" Cole said as he wiped blood from his lip.

"Not the point, asshole!" Levi said. "Bet she doesn't know about all that, does she?" Levi jerked a thumb toward Marie. He didn't bother meeting Jesse's glare from where she stood next to Marie.

"What? That Jesse and I were together for about a minute?" Cole answered around Cade, who had moved between the two men.

"Nope. Not about that. About the crazy stuff you did." Cole winced in response. "What? You didn't advertise that you're a little jacked up? Did you tell her about running Jesse's ex off the road? No?"

Cole held his hands up in a half-surrender, but Levi

wouldn't be stopped. "How about the times you let yourself in Jesse's house? Didn't think she'd tell me that? She did. You scared the hell out of her, you creepy bastard."

Marie watched the exchange from a detached place. She noticed how Cole's chest heaved, working to control his rage as Levi said horrible things about him in front of everyone. His fists tightened at his side, and he looked like he was about to pound Levi into the ground.

"That's enough, Levi." Jesse stepped between the men and leaned into Levi. Through clenched teeth she quietly hissed, "Don't you dare do this in front of everyone. The kids are here. Marie is a guest!"

"He nailed a dead cat to Drake's door! He's a stalker!" Levi said, despite Jesse's warning.

At that, Marie's stomach turned. It was one thing to think he and Jesse briefly dated, but another to think he stalked her. Or that he hurt an animal. Marie listened to the hateful words Cole and Levi spit out at each other for a few more minutes before turning to walk back to the house. She dug around in Jesse's purse until she found keys. She sent a quick text to let Jesse know she'd taken her truck, and in no time she was making her way down a gravel road pointed toward her rented cabin.

She was nothing but a trail of gravel dust by the time that Cole heard all he could stand and smashed his fist into Levi's mouth. Marie missed the way Cole roared when he accused Levi of standing in the way of his happiness when everyone else around them found their happy ending. She didn't see when Jake came flying around the house in time to try and talk Cole down. When Cole landed a punch on Jake, he wound up in cuffs, being hauled in to sleep off the rage before Jesse bailed him out the next day.

Marie ignored the phone calls the next morning as well as the knock on her door. She heard an engine and knew either Jesse or Levi was getting their truck from her cabin. She had zero interest in peopling, which included one person in particular.

Her phone dinged with a message.

How goes it in the woods? - H.C.

I've about had all I can take of the peace and quiet. Marie answered, enjoying the irony. Peace and quiet had not exactly been on the radar the last few weeks.

Really? That didn't take long. I knew you couldn't hack it out there. Crazy lady. - H.C.

That makes me want to stay longer to prove you wrong, but I think I'll head for home in the next few days. Time to get back to the grind. - Marie

Sorry it didn't work out. - H.C.

Me, too. Hey, we need to talk soon. Can you meet up? - Marie

Sure, I've got a few days off next week. - H.C.

Perfect. Message me later. Love you. - Marie

Love you, too. - H.C.

When Cole knocked on her door that evening, Marie nearly jumped out of her skin. As the hours ticked by, she figured he had enough sense not to come around. She gave it a few minutes thinking he'd get the point and walk away. However, she reminded herself, she wasn't dealing with the usual suspects. She shivered at the term. Nope. Leave it to her to find a stalker. *Sounds about right*, she said to herself as she walked to the door. She unlocked it and leaned against the frame.

"I didn't think you were going to answer," Cole said quietly.

"I didn't think you were going to go away, so…" Marie answered, stepping back from the door.

"Can we talk for a little bit?" he asked before stepping into the doorway.

"Funny, I didn't think cat-murdering stalkers stopped to ask permission before doing whatever they wanted."

Cole sighed. "It's not like that. I mean, I did accidentally kill the cat—and do something awful with it—but that's not the whole story. Can I come in?"

She shrugged. "Come in. I need a drink. You?" She watched for his nod before pouring two tall glasses of bourbon.

Cole sat beside her and downed his glass. He placed it on a coaster and turned his body toward hers. "I've done some things I'm not proud of. But I didn't stalk Jesse." He ran his hands through his hair. His elbows rested on his knees as he explained what happened. "I told you what life was like for me growing up. I can't stomach men mistreating women. Did Jesse ever tell you how her ex-husband treated her?"

Marie shrugged, not really remembering much other than Jesse had been unhappy and got out.

"He made her feel like dirt. Like she was a crap mother, a crap wife, and a crap excuse for a human being. She used to get sick to her stomach before having to meet with him to get the kids. When she talked with him on the phone in the beginning, she told me her hands would shake." He continued. "He needed to be knocked down a few pegs."

"But he still lives up near St. Louis, right? What did you do, drive all the way up there and…" her voice trailed off as Cole didn't blink an eye. "You did. You drove two hours to mess with him?"

Cole nodded solemnly. "I was trying to send Drake a message. He changed his tune after a while, so it wasn't ineffective."

"I remember he was a huge dick, but I have to say, this sounds pretty screwed up," Marie said, rubbing the spot between her eyes.

"Agreed. And the cat was an accident. I ran over his girlfriend's cat. I was trying to scare the hell out of him, so I, uh… I nailed it to the door and left a note that he was going to be next."

"For the love," she whispered.

"I know. That was pretty screwed up." He shrugged his shoulders.

Marie snorted with laughter and clamped both her hands over her mouth. Her eyes swam with tears and her shoulders shook. Cole shifted back against the back of the couch and watched her in confusion.

"This vacation has definitely worked out differently than I ever imagined. I mean, I wreck my car, meet a mountain man, have the most terrific sex of my life—kudos, by the way—and he ends up a cat-murdering, ex-husband punisher. I thought I was going to take naps and read some trashy romance novels. I feel like I'm living in one." Marie fell back against a pillow and turned her body toward Cole.

He pulled her feet onto his lap and began rubbing one. "Listen. I didn't mean to complicate things so much. I wanted to let you know I'm leaving tomorrow."

"Where are you going?" she asked, determined not to relax no matter what magic he was working on her feet.

"A fire out in Texas. Got the call this afternoon. I'll be gone for two weeks, so you'll be back to your normal life by the time I'm back." He waited for her nod before continuing. "Listen, Marie. I didn't want last night to be the lasting impression of me. Levi and I were overdue to air things out. I would've preferred it not be in front of an entire group of people, but it is what it is, I guess," he said with a shrug of a shoulder.

Marie was stunned for a second by the mix of emotions she felt. This man was obviously bad news. He had no place in her life beyond the mountain. She'd spent the whole day planning on never seeing him again. Why, then, did she feel disappointed that he was leaving town?

Cole gave her feet a squeeze and stood. Marie watched as he turned and held his hand out for her to join him. She took the open invitation to his arms and laid her head against his chest.

"I'm not really sure what to say here," Marie answered truthfully.

"Me either. I'm so glad we met," Cole said. "I haven't connected like this with anyone in a really long time."

Marie reached up and pressed a kiss to his lips. She let herself enjoy one last time the sensation of his arms enveloping her. He might be a loose cannon with a lot of baggage, but when he held her like this, she felt protected. She took a step back and out of his arms once the moment had passed.

"Take care, Cole. Be safe." She led the way to the door.

"I will. Good luck getting back into the swing of things in St. Louis." Cole pressed a kiss to the top of her head and walked out.

Marie locked the door behind him and leaned against it as she danced along the edge of wanting to replay everything that had happened over the last few weeks or make a terrific effort to block it all out completely. She was in her own head so much that she hadn't noticed that his truck engine roared to life outside but he didn't pull out of the drive.

When the knock sounded on her door, she let out a shriek that nearly raised the dead. Marie jerked it open with one hand over her heart as Cole filled the doorway.

Little lines formed at the edges of his amused eyes. "Sorry."

"By the expression on your face, I'm not sure I believe that," Marie replied.

"I don't want to leave it like this. Will you go someplace with me?"

Marie looked at her watch. "Right now? Where?"

Cole shut the door behind him to block out the cold air. "You'll have to wait and see. It's chilly out. Better bundle up."

Marie exhaled and weighed her options. She could throw him out now and basically rip the Bandaid off at once, or prolong this goodbye. She grumbled under her breath as she turned to walk back to the bedroom to get properly dressed.

"We aren't hiking, are we? I took all that crap back to Amy," she called down the hallway.

"No, no hiking this time." Cole chuckled when he heard her hiss as she thanked God. He went to the hallway closet and pulled out a stack of blankets that Ryan stocked in all the cabins. By the time Marie walked out her front door, he had stored them away in his truck.

He held the truck door open as she climbed in. She cranked the heat up to full blast and dared him to adjust it when he got in.

"Where are we headed?"

He glanced her way. "It's a surprise. Don't be a pest," he fake scolded.

Marie thought back to her initial impression of southern Illinois on her eventful arrival. She'd never profess to be an outdoors enthusiast, but she had slightly relaxed her position. At least enough to appreciate the beauty of her surroundings.

"I still can't get over the stars here," she said.

"Don't have the same view at home?" he asked, curious about her life in the city.

She shook her head slightly. "They're dimmer, somehow."

"The lights reflect into the sky, so you can't see the stars as easily," he confirmed.

"Makes sense," she said. "Good grief, how high up are we climbing?" she asked rubbing her hand over her stomach at the increase in incline.

"Just a bit more. It'll be worth it," he said, giving her knee a squeeze before returning his hand to the wheel. "Gets a little narrow here. Can you reach out and fold the mirror in?" he said as he rolled down his own window. She watched what he did and repeated it on the other side.

Marie was relieved when Cole parked the truck.

"So, where are we?" she asked, hopping down from the truck as he reached in the second row of seats and pulled out blanket after blanket.

"Wamble Mountain," he said, waggling his eyebrows.

"I thought our places were on the mountain," she asked.

He shrugged. "There's more than one. Here, follow me." Cole threw the blankets in the bed of his truck and hopped up into the bed.

Marie answered in an exasperated tone. "Cole, the freaking truck is too tall. What do you mean, 'follow me'?"

He laughed and reached his hand out to pull her up as she stepped on the top of his tire. "Fussy, fussy. First you don't want my help. Then you do want my help. How am I supposed to keep up?"

Marie rolled her eyes and then gasped as she took in her surroundings.

"Cole, this is beautiful!" Marie looked out from their perch in the bed of his truck over a rock ledge. Before her she saw lights in five bunches.

"Pretty, isn't it? Those are all the little surrounding towns. This was a favorite hangout in my younger days. Well, pretty much in everyone's younger days. It's where the teenagers come to make out," he grinned.

"Ah, I get it. Good ambiance."

"Agreed," he said, pulling Marie down into the nest of blankets he had arranged. "Pretty lights, for sure. Something about this spot always helped me adjust my perspective on things when I was younger. Haven't visited in a while. I was overdue," he added quietly.

Marie gave his hand a squeeze as his lips brushed against her neck. "The real show is about to start," he said as he glanced at his watch and raised goosebumps on her skin. "I wanted to surprise you with this, but I wasn't sure you'd let me after last night."

Her pulse quickened as she braced herself for his hands on her body, but he didn't move from their position. A thud of disappointment settled in her until he pointed up into the sky. "Watch."

She glanced up and saw the beginnings of a meteor shower. Her breath caught in her throat as she took it in. The combination of sensations was nearly overwhelming. The cold air against her face, the warm man against her body, the inky sky and streaks of light all mixed together into butterflies in her stomach. Most of all, she was torn by the two truths she knew down to the bottom of her soul. First, this man was an absolute train wreck, and second, he made her feel things she had never felt before. Right or wrong, she wanted him.

Marie turned away from the sky and straddled Cole's legs. His eyes burned into hers as she pressed her body against his. Cole gathered a blanket from the bed and wrapped it against her back, not knowing she was, at that point, burning from the inside out, impervious to the chill in the air.

Her hands caressed his shoulders and neck as her lips teased against his. Cole's hands gripped her ass and ground her body somehow closer. A groan left her lips as he started a rhythm that she liked.

Cole nipped at her throat, and the scruff of his day-old beard rasped against her skin. He moaned as his hand snaked beneath her shirt to cradle her naked breast. He grunted his approval at this little surprise, and his mouth became more urgent against hers. She could almost read the question in his mind as his fingers trailed down to find the answer. A laugh escaped her nearly trapped lips at his response. Beneath the shining stars, Cole and Marie did the old make-out mountain proud.

ten

COLE STOOD ON THE PORCH of the land owner's house on a hillside as flames engulfed the neighboring home downhill and across the way.

"Sir, this doesn't feel right," Cole said into the radio to his supervisor.

"I know, son. Let's just go and get it done. Do your best and hope to hell we get out of here."

Dread settled in Cole's gut, but there wasn't a thing he could do about it. The gully was about the width of a two-lane interstate. He knew it was literally the worst place to be in a fire. It's exactly where it would funnel. The trees were fuel for the fire, and heat rises. The wind kept switching, and embers were flying over the fire-line to the opposite side.

There was no water, no foam to protect the house, and no aircraft.

"Sir, this is your absolute last chance to haul ass and get out of here," Cole yelled to the homeowner as he walked in his direction.

"I'm not leaving my property!" the man yelled back.

"Got it. I want you to go inside the house and not come out until the absolute last minute."

The man looked terrified. "Go inside? Isn't that the worst place for me to be?"

"No, the flames aren't likely to be what kills you. The gas fumes will kill you before the flames. You know how soldiers wear gas masks? Same thing. Hold your breath as long as you can. I'm getting out of here. Good luck to you, sir."

"I'm a danged finger-pointer now. I thought these days were over," he muttered as he tried to be compassionate for the homeowner whose house he'd been defending. There was a level of stupid that he just couldn't fix. The man should have evacuated at least a day ago. At that moment, a Chinook came into view. The bucket on that thing held around one thousand gallons and was a very welcome sight. Cole pulled out his radio. "Get me that Chinook," he said to dispatch. He waited anxiously for the dispatcher to put him through. Cole explained his position, but the pilot couldn't see through the smoke.

"I can't tell if this is it, but it's as close as I think I can get it blind. I've got to wait 'til the crew leaves." Cole watched as the crew fled the house and ran into a plowed field. He could hear them on the radio but couldn't seem them for all the smoke as it worsened by the second.

The homeowner stood beside Cole and sobbed as the pilot dropped water on the neighboring house. The canyon was about a quarter of a mile wide, and Cole could see the fire coming.

Cole looked back at the man one more time before stepping down off the porch, willing him to come.

The man raked his hands through his hair. "I'll come with you! Wait!" he said, running into the house. Cole followed and saw the man grabbing picture frames off the wall.

"I'll help. Move fast!" Cole moved quickly through the house filling his arms with pictures frames. They threw them in the truck and heard the crackle of glass. "Still better than what the fire would do. You made a good choice," he said, hoping for a conciliatory tone for the poor man. He grabbed the man by the arm and nearly shoved him into the truck as he stood rooted to the spot watching the fire move closer.

"It moves in chunks," he explained as the man stared out the window. "It comes in at one angle, shifts clockwise. It doesn't envelop everything at once."

The man turned to look out the back window as the flames devoured one corner of his house. Cole pulled over as soon as he was a safe enough distance away. He and the man watched as the house was lost within ten minutes.

"FORTY YEARS I lived in that house," the man said. He wiped at his face with a hanky he fished from his pocket. "I carried Hazel over the threshold the day we married. Brought babies home to that house," he said, his voice hitching with emotion. "Hell, one was born at home. That was John, number three. Hazel used to joke that she sneezed and there he was!" he said with a watery smile. Cole listened as the man shared memories as they drove back to the group of trucks stationed nearby. "She's been gone for nearly twenty years now. That woman was the love of my life. Still hurts," he said. A lump formed in Cole's throat as the old fellow rambled on. "Tell you what, son. You ever find a woman who feels like air—you got to have her to breathe right— you don't let her get away," he said as his voice tapered off.

In his mind's eye Cole saw Marie curled in his arms that last time, flushed from making love in the bed of his truck of all places. He knew he didn't deserve to have had her in his life at all. She deserved better than someone as utterly messed up as he was. He'd screwed up so many times with his temper and impulsivity. He didn't deserve to have a woman like that.

Marie was like a firework. Unstable, explosive, but the most incredibly beautiful thing he'd ever seen. His heart told him that it would never work. He was being stupid. They'd only known each other for a few weeks. She had her life in the city and he lived alone in the woods, haunted by the ghost of his dead fiancée.

After Cole got the old man delivered where he could get checked out and contact family or friends, he settled in to fill out his log sheet. He was supposed to be writing down all his actions to justify them. In the end it was a success because nobody got hurt, but he hated that the man's house couldn't be saved.

Cole tamped down the feelings swirling around his gut. He had another week left of fighting fires, and he literally couldn't risk him or his men getting hurt because of the little, dark-headed distraction clawing at his mind.

eleven

EXHAUSTED MENTALLY AND physically, Cole made a change to his itinerary at the airport. Instead of driving back to southern Illinois, he got a room at a hotel. He wasn't about to call Marie in the middle of the night after all the ugly things Levi had shared about him. He'd wait and surprise her the next day and hope she wanted to see him. They'd slept together that last night on the mountain, he thought with a shiver, but that was a goodbye. It didn't mean all was forgiven.

It wasn't tough to find Marie's address. Nothing is private anymore, thanks to the internet. Cole pulled in front of her condo and saw that her car was parked in the driveway. Sucking in a big breath, he knocked and listened as footsteps moved closer to the door. A smile spread over his face and was quickly replaced by a stone cold expression.

It took him about two seconds to pull the guy in his boxers into a headlock while he tossed the man against the exterior wall.

"What the hell, man?" the guy yelled as Cole put pressure against his throat.

Cole hissed, "Who are you?" into the man's ear.

"Cole!" Marie screamed. "Get your hands off of my son!" she said, slipping quickly between Cole and the man. The *young* man, Cole suddenly noticed.

Cole stood immobilized while Marie all but ripped his head from his shoulders. He even missed many of the insults she threw at him. His brain was on repeat with the words, "*Her son? She has a grown son.*" The mantra repeated in question and answer form until she wore herself out from exhaustion as she railed against him.

Cole picked back up on what she was saying when the words "call the police" floated into the air. By that time, Marie had scared the living hell out of her son, and he had either retreated to another room or had been ordered into it. Cole slumped down a little to bring his head closer to her level.

"Marie? That's your son?" he asked, the fog clearing from his brain. "I'm so sorry!"

Her face filled with emotion. First rage, and then tears. "Yes, you idiot. That's my son, Holden. You stay here, asshole. I'll be right back." She slammed the door, and Cole guessed she was either checking on her son or getting her gun.

"Holden?" he asked her, still dazed, yet surprised by the unusual name when she emerged from the door unarmed.

With her hand fisted on her hip, she arched an eyebrow. "Yes, *Catcher in the Rye* is one of my favorite books. I named him that halfway to spite his father who probably never bothered to crack a book," she said, throwing her hands up in the air as she stepped in front of him and sat down on her front step.

He followed suit and sat a stair below her. "I'm so sorry. All I saw was a nearly naked man at your door," Cole explained, hearing the weakness in his argument.

"It's my door, Cole. What makes you think it's your business who's on the other side of it?" she asked, genuinely confused. Sure, she'd done nothing but think of him over the past few weeks that she'd been home, but he needed to learn the definition of the word boundary.

He turned to look at her with a world of hurt in his eyes. "Marie, why didn't you tell me you had a child? We shared so much of our lives, but you didn't mention a son. I know we didn't go through a detailed history, but that's a pretty big thing to leave out!"

His question bypassed all her common sense and good raising. She jumped to her feet and pointed a finger in his face. "You were supposed to be a fling, Cole! A fling! You are an excellent screw, but you live on the top of a mountain in the middle of nowhere. I never thought you'd turn up in my real life!" She nearly screamed those last words and felt herself grow red in the face when a neighbor walked by with a yapping chihuahua tethered to a leash.

"It is more to me than that," Cole answered. "I haven't stopped thinking about you. I got caught in a fire out there. Closest I've ever come to really getting in some trouble…" he said, looking down as the memories of that fateful moment washed over him. Marie put her hand on his arm before she could stop herself. Cole continued, "I met a man who described his late wife as the air he breathed. He told me if I ever met a woman that felt like air, like she was my everything, I couldn't let her go. It's you, Marie."

She shook her head, rejecting his words. "Cole, you just tried to beat the hell out of my son. This can't…" she said, gesturing between them, "*this* can't be a thing."

"There's something you don't know." He ran his hands through his hair as he struggled to put the right words together. "I was engaged once. We got together right after high school, and before long, we were engaged. It was stupid. We were just kids." His voice faded off. "Once I enlisted, we didn't get to see each other much. She stayed here, and I was gone. First to California, then deployed. It sucked, and things were weird. You're not exactly the same person at twenty-one that you are at eighteen, but we were stuck."

He quirked an eyebrow at Marie's derisive snort in agreement. "I kept my separation day a secret because I wanted to surprise her when I got home. I had flowers, chocolates, everything but the boombox over my head, ya know?" He looked at her, begging her to listen to him, although she ought to be running him off her steps with a baseball bat.

"I knocked on the door and waited. Her car was in the driveway and lights were on. I knew she was home, but it took a while. When the door opened it was a guy, not my wife. She was a few steps behind him, like he was going to shield her or something.

"His shoes were off, hair rumpled. It's not like it took a brain surgeon to figure out what the hell had been going on. I lost it. I didn't even have to land a punch before that coward was out the door. Mandy went ballistic. She blamed all of it on me. I left her alone too much," she said. "I left her stranded out in the country without any friends. She was young and beautiful and wasting it all on a piece of trash like me. That one stung." Cole shook his head a little as he played the scene back in his mind for the thousandth time.

"She had been drinking, and her words were a little slurred. She ranted on and on about needing someone better than me, someone that was home and who could actually communicate. Mandy bitched and bitched about how I never talked to her beyond small talk and that's why she was bored with me. She just kept on and on, and I lost it. I told her what she could do and how she could do it. She grabbed her purse and tried to leave. I grabbed her; I knew she was too drunk to drive. The stink coming off her was awful, you know that stale whiskey smell?"

Marie nodded, and he continued. "She was hell-bent on leaving. I looked around at how the house was trashed. I was the only one getting a paycheck. She had wanted to stay home. She was supposed to be taking classes that I was paying for, but she kept flaking out and quitting. I resented the hell out of her, honestly. So, I let her go. The weather had kicked up a little bit, and the roads were slick. She was trashed and hit a tree. Died at the scene. All because I didn't man up and make her stay."

"Cole, if she was blaming you for everything, there's no way she would've stayed." She was livid with him but placed a hand on his back in a gesture of comfort. "Her idiocy and death isn't your fault. Not if you tried your best." Marie knew firsthand that you couldn't make someone change if they didn't want to.

"I tried to get Kevin to stop drinking even before we got married. At that point, like you guys, we were really young. At first it wasn't that big of a deal. He'd get tanked, and I'd be the driver. He was working long hours and justified that it was the only way he could relax. I was stupid enough to buy it. Then, like you and I already talked about, it just got worse from there."

Cole put his hand on her shoulder and gave it a squeeze, his silent thanks that she let him talk about Mandy. That was something he didn't share with anyone. "Is your ex your son's father?"

"Yes. I didn't realize I was pregnant the night I left. It was about three weeks later when I figured it out. God, the tears I cried over that one. All I could think about was being tied to that asshole for the rest of my life. It wasn't until I started showing later on that I realized there could be a lot of good to come out of this.

"Holden came along, and my world was better. I mean, it was hard as hell working crappy jobs and raising a baby, but my parents helped so much. I don't know how people make it when they don't have some kind of support system in place.

"I haven't ever told him any details about Kevin, or that his dad was in prison in the next town over. I sure as hell haven't told him that Kevin's been released," she said, rubbing the tension from her neck unconsciously.

Cole replaced her hand with his. "Hasn't he been curious about who his father is?" Cole asked tentatively.

Marie shrugged. "Yes, it's made him nuts over the years. By the time he was old enough to handle an answer, I gave him one so gross that he didn't ask about it for a while. I told him it was a one-night stand and I never got his name."

Cole grinned and shook his head back and forth. "I know. Dishonest, but I didn't want him to be ashamed. Well, *more* ashamed. I'd rather him think I had screwed around than know he had a convict for a father. More than that, I didn't want to share him with that low-life."

"Understandable," he said, reaching for her hand.

She stood up and wiped her hands down the front of her jeans. "Listen, Cole. I care about you more than I want to. Wait, let me finish," she said when he started to interrupt. "The part of you that isn't jacked up is absolutely awesome."

Cole winced at her words as they landed like darts in his chest. "I'm sorry, but it's not acceptable to jump somebody because you don't like your perception of what's going on.

Even if it reeks of déjà vu. I hate that you've been hurt before, and I hate that your fiancée was killed in an accident, leaving you with guilt. You're not guilty for that," she said, grabbing his forearm and giving it a squeeze. "That was her stupidity, not yours. On all counts."

"Thank you for that, but Marie, I think you're wrong on this. There's something here," he said.

She saw a flash of vulnerability go across his face, but she was determined to be firm. "I'm sorry, Cole. You should go now."

Cole released a deep breath. He had already made a mess of things with Marie. He wasn't going to exacerbate the situation by not leaving when asked. Cole gave a small smile and pulled the keys from his pocket. He watched her stand on the porch with a flat expression as he pulled away. When his truck was no longer visible, Marie took a deep breath and went back inside.

To HER SURPRISE, her son wasn't in his room like she guessed he'd be. He was practically vibrating with anger in the front room.

"Holden, are you hurt? You said you were okay," she said, moving in to check him for injuries.

He rounded on his mother for the first time in his life. "You know who my father is?" he said, his voice thick with accusation.

Marie's eyes widened. "You listened to my conversation?" she asked, her voice shrill in her own ears.

"Your conversation with the head case that slammed me into the damned wall? Yeah, Mom, I did."

"Watch your mouth!" she said, her finger inches from his face. She had taken a firm hand with Holden from the very beginning. She knew it would be no time before he was bigger than she was, so she did her best to teach him respect from the get-go.

He didn't even flinch. "You've known all along, and you didn't bother to tell me who my own father is. I can't believe you!" he yelled.

Marie took a bracing breath. The conversation she'd been dreading for twenty-one years wouldn't be possible unless they got a handle on their emotions. "I'll talk with you about this the instant you get ahold of yourself. I'll be in the kitchen when you're ready to speak respectfully to me." She turned on her heel and stood in front of the tea kettle debating on a cup of Earl Grey or a shot of whiskey. After consulting her watch, she went with the tea.

twelve

Halfway through her second cup, Holden came into the room and took a seat at the table. She decided to let him start the questioning and was determined to wait him out. Marie watched her son out of the corner of her eye and marveled at what an awesome kid he was. Holden was twenty-one years old, a senior in college, and a soon-to-be mechanical engineer. He was independent, funny, and smart as a whip. He was a little over six feet tall, had a head full of dark, curly hair, and had Marie's green eyes. *He's mature enough to handle this*, she said to herself, almost as a prayer.

After a big breath and a partially dirty look, Holden said, "Please tell me about my father."

A lead balloon settled in her stomach. *I was hoping*

for closed-answer questions, she thought. "Your father and I dated in high school and married right after. He was a big drinker, and it didn't take long for me to realize it wasn't going to work," she said, skipping over some very important details. *There's no reason he has to know everything*, Marie rationalized.

"At about the six-month point I left, filed for divorce, and never saw him again." She didn't miss the tiny scoff Holden gave. "What? You think it's easy to make excellent decisions at eighteen? Can you see yourself married and divorced at your age? What about a parent of a toddler?"

Marie took a steadying breath, and Holden didn't say a word. "Your father didn't contest the divorce. He was remarried soon after."

"What's his name?" he asked without making eye contact.

"Kevin Von Arb. There's more, though," she said as he interrupted.

"Nice. I don't even have his last name?" Holden said accusingly.

She narrowed her eyes in warning. "I changed my name back when the divorce was final and had yours match mine. I knew I'd be raising you alone, and it would be easier with school and stuff if our names matched." Marie chose to ignore his eye roll.

"Holden, I haven't even gotten to the worst part yet. Be patient, please," Marie petitioned. "Your father had a terrible drinking problem. He was arrested several times for hitting his new wife." She paused and let this soak in slowly as her son's face filled with disgust. "Once, he hit his wife and she fell and hit her head, and it killed her, son. Your father was charged with manslaughter and sent to prison."

Marie cut her eyes to the patio door to give her son the minute of privacy he needed to process the awful news she shared. Holden wasn't one to shed tears easily, but she saw them gathering in his eyes. "I didn't want you to be ashamed or ridiculed by his actions. It may or may not have been the right thing to do, but I felt it was right. I definitely didn't want you growing up visiting him in prison. He doesn't even know about you, and I'd be happy if it always stayed that way."

Holden gave his eyes a quick swipe and rose to get a cup of coffee from the pot Marie had made him. "Unbelievable. All my life I've been obsessed with wondering who my father is, and it turns out he's a murdering piece of trash."

"Like I said, I haven't been in direct contact with him since the night I left him, so I don't know what he's like. That's been over twenty years ago. I have to hope that her death was accidental, however from the article in the newspaper that reported the trial, the abuse was common." Marie sipped her tea and wished she was able to tell him some other story.

"Holden, I want you to know that this doesn't have to change anything. You're an incredible young man. Smart, funny," she stood, pulling her son into a hug, "gorgeous like me," she teased, earning a slight smile. "This doesn't change a thing about who you are."

"I wish it were different," he said, resting his head on hers for a second.

"Me, too, kid." Marie stepped out of the hug and took a deep breath. "Want some breakfast?" she asked, looking again at her watch. "Brunch, I mean?"

"Yeah, may as well. While you're cooking, tell me about the psycho that just placed my indent into the wall."

Marie's eyes jerked to her son and then the front door in a panic. "Just kidding, Mom. But man, who the hell was that?"

She took a steadying breath before launching into what parts of that particular story she was willing to share with her grown son. "That was Cole. We met while I was in southern Illinois on my vacation from reality."

"And why did he slam me against the wall?" Holden asked. "Do you have the very worst taste in men, or what?"

She plopped the plate that would hold his scrambled eggs in front of him with a little more force than necessary. "Probably." Marie paused with a hip leaned against the table. "I think he's actually one of the good ones, but his impulse control is nil. That's more than I'm prepared to deal with right now."

Holden winced. "Yeah, good call," he said, rubbing a hand over his neck where Cole had grabbed him.

"Holden?" She waited until her son was looking her in the eye. "Leave this thing with Kevin alone, okay? He's dangerous." Her tea turned to ash in her mouth as she watched her son nod but saw the lack of commitment in his eyes.

thirteen

*F*UNNY HOW IT ALL COMES DOWN *to pictures*, he thought. Cole's fingers brushed against the strings on his guitar as the notes were nearly drowned out by the crackling of the fire in front of him. Most of his nights were spent on the back deck as winter reluctantly gave way to spring. The air had lost its bite and tiny blooms were daring to appear on the bare trees.

Of all his possessions, Cole only had two things that meant the world to him. One was a photo of Cole and Marie on his phone, the other was a childhood photo with his sister and grandpa. The rest of his stuff could be gone in an instant and he'd never even miss it.

The notes morphed into chords as "Pictures of You"

sounded against the lonely night in Cole's deep drawl, his eyes shut as he gave over to the therapy of music.

"Never took you for a man that would listen to The Cure," Ryan said, jolting Cole from his sad reverie. The only hint Ryan had that he had taken Cole by surprise was a tic in his jaw as the music abruptly stopped. "'Course I almost didn't recognize it with that Tennessee accent of yours," Ryan said, reaching his hand out in time to catch the bottle of beer Cole had tossed in the direction of his nose.

"This a thing now?" Cole asked, gesturing to Ryan as he took a seat in the patio chair a few feet away and popped the cap on the bottle.

"What? Dropping by?" he asked, smirking at Cole's nod. "You started it." The two sipped in companionable silence and watched the flames dance against the night. "I didn't even know you played, man. You're good."

Cole half nodded in acceptance of the compliment. "Started years ago. Gives me something to do."

Ryan watched him and decided there was no point beating around the bush. "Well, I'd better do as I'm told and get to the point," he said, stretching his legs out in front of him. "Amy sent me up here to check on you."

"What are you talking about?" Cole asked, picking up his guitar again, more to fidget than to play.

"Dude, we've been getting night time concerts for a few weeks now. At first she loved it, and I'll admit, it got me lucky a few nights more than our usual scheduled weekly screw. Now, she's worried over you, and it's ruining my chances 'til I fix you." Ryan softly laughed.

Cole raked his hand through his hair. "First off, man, you're welcome. Second, I had no idea you could hear me at your place. Sorry."

"Sounds carry right down the ridge. Not much to stop it but the trees, and they're bare. Plus, like I said, it's pretty and worked out well for me. No worries, there," Ryan answered, tossing a hand in Cole's direction. "Really, though, she sent me to snoop. You doing alright?" he asked, taking a long pull off his beer.

"How is Amy? The kid?" Cole asked.

"Nice try. They're fine. How's Marie?" Ryan asked, watching his friend closely.

Cole dug two more drinks out of the cooler and passed one along. Seemed like a perfect night to get hammered. He wasn't due out to California for another thirty-six hours. "I'm not sure. Haven't talked to her since I completely screwed everything up."

The laugh that had busted out of Ryan died on his lips as Cole's cutthroat glare iced the blood in his veins. "Oh man, Cole. You really like her."

He nodded once as he tilted the bottle to his lips. When he settled into silence again, Ryan flirted with the idea of bailing instead of dragging the information out of his non-communicative friend. Ryan let loose a resigned sigh. His wife would kill him if he came home without details.

"I'd ask what you did, but I'm kind of afraid you'll kill me and throw me in a ditch," he said, going with humor.

"Nothing too serious; put her kid in a headlock," Cole answered in a gruff voice.

A fine mist of beer sprayed into the air around them as Ryan sputtered. "You what?" He dragged his arm across his face.

"Yeah. I knocked on her door, and a guy answered in his boxers. I had him pinned against the wall in a second." He put his guitar and drink down and leaned his elbows on his knees, his face in his hands. "I swear, man," he said, his voice slightly muffled, "it was just like coming home and finding Mandy cheating again."

Cole righted himself in his chair and picked the bottle up. "I was engaged once," he started, but stopped when Ryan held up his hand.

"You told me about that one night," he said quietly and looked quickly back to the flames. This conversation was hard enough. He didn't need Cole rehashing all that unnecessarily.

Cole heaved a sigh and looked up at the stars. "It's like I lose all control of my body when I get that pissed. Instinct or something."

Ryan didn't breathe a word. There comes a point when you have to own your actions, experience be hanged. *Easy for you to say, you've had it pretty easy*, he scolded himself.

"Anyway, I threw that guy... that kid," he amended, "against the wall and had my head handed to me by Marie." He leveled a look at Ryan. "She's got a serious mouth on her," he said with a grin. "I'm not joking. I haven't had my ass chewed out like that since the Marines. After she calmed down a little bit, she told me more about her marriage and raising her son on her own." He shook his head slightly. "God, she's a tough little thing."

"So, she threw you out on your ear after that?" Ryan asked, wondering how Cole could be so stupid. "And, how old is this kid?"

"He's twenty-one. If I had hesitated even a second, I would've noticed that. I just saw a nearly naked man. And, yeah, we talked for a little while and then she dismissed me."

"Dismissed you?"

"Basically. I deserved it, too." A heavy pause hung in the air. "What the hell is wrong with me?" Cole said in a low voice.

"Eh, I could go on for hours..." Ryan said, hitting his friend on the knee with the gloves he'd been holding on his lap. "You look awful. This has got you torn up, hasn't it?"

Cole nodded. "I can't eat. I'm not sleeping worth a crap. She's all I think about," he said, upending the bottle. He set it down and reached toward the cooler but decided against it. It wasn't worth the hangover after all, and he already felt exhausted.

Unsure if further conversation was going to help his friend or get himself punched in the face, Ryan decided to tread carefully. "Have you called her?"

Cole shook his head slowly. "She made it pretty clear she can't be with a nut job."

"She called you that?" Ryan asked, his opinion of Marie lowering a notch or two.

"Not in so many words. She isn't down for anything serious, and certainly not with someone like me."

Ryan shifted in his seat a little, moving where he could better see his friend in the light of the fire. "Listen, you've had some horrible luck. I'm not kidding. But this self-deprecating business has got to go. You can be mule headed all you want, but let me tell you what you're clearly forgetting. Your upbringing was a friggin' catastrophe. You grew up with a horrible example for what a man should be. The hair-trigger temper thing is a risk, certainly, but have you ever hit a woman?"

Cole flushed at the question. "Of course not!" he nearly growled.

"Exactly. The idea pisses you off, I can see that. Fine. That's not exactly a commendation of what it takes to be a good man—that's setting the bar low—but the point is, that you'd never do it. You freaking dismantled bombs in the Marines."

"Some might say that proves that I have a screw loose," Cole said, tapping his temple with a finger but settling down a bit.

"Bull, Cole, it was good money. You took a job that required focus and bravery, to the point of near-insanity." Ryan kicked his feet up on a stack of logs for the fire pit. "And, look what you've accomplished. How else could you have built a place like this by your age? And, I've seen pictures from the old days. I remember that big, honking ring your fiancée had..." he said, thinking back to the huge ring that Mandy had flashed every chance she'd been given. "This is morbid as hell, but did you get that back?" Ryan asked quietly.

Cole shook his head. "No, man. Her family needed that more than I did. They thought all of it was my fault anyway." He shrugged.

"See? Another point. If you were as ruthless and horrible as you make yourself out to be, you would have blamed her for all of it and hocked the ring. What did you do instead? Paid for a service fit for a celebrity and set her family up to boot."

Ryan watched as Cole visibly grew uncomfortable. "My point, Cole, is that you're not the monster you make yourself out to be. All this 'she deserves more' crap is a waste of breath. Your temper is off the charts, but more than that, I think it's your freakin' impulse control. I can think of about ten points in the conversation you could've rightfully bashed my face in, but here I sit, pretty as ever, teeth intact."

Cole looked Ryan dead in the eye. "What do I do?"

"Don't give up. If you think she's it, don't give up. Show her you're more than a caveman."

Cole felt his mouth lift in a grin at the reference. Marie had called him caveman, and he'd loved it. "Thanks, man. I'll call her when I get back from California."

"Three weeks?" Ryan asked, standing and pulling on his gloves.

"Just two. You okay looking in?" he asked, thankful that his friend could check on his property while he was out of town.

"Sure thing, man," Ryan said, slapping his back in an awkward man-hug. "Be safe."

"Will do. And, thanks."

Ryan jerked his head in acknowledgement. "I'm an expert, what can I say?"

"Yeah, I bet that's just what Amy would say," Cole said with a laugh.

Ryan wiggled his eyebrows and walked around the house. Cole stayed in his chair until the fire died out thinking of how he was going to convince Marie he was a risk worth taking.

fourteen

HOLDEN SAT, DUMBFOUNDED, STARING at the information on the screen. In a matter of minutes after getting back to his apartment he'd found his father's whereabouts. Between internet searches and social media, it was easy enough to research. "*Manslaughter*," he said quietly to himself. "It's disgusting, but it's not the same as murderone," he rationalized. "I don't understand why Mom never mentioned it. I'm in college; I can handle this."

The phone rang twice before a gravely, sleep-filled voice answered on the other end. "Hello?" he rasped.

Holden glanced at his watch again, 11:00 AM. He was on a break between classes and was surprised anyone would be asleep. His heart beat in his ears. He was talking to his father.

"Um, hello. This is Holden, is this Kevin Von Arb?"

"Who the hell did you say it is? What time is it?" the man growled as Holden heard items being shuffled around in the background.

"Is this Kevin Von Arb?"

"Yes."

Holden took a deep breath. "I'm Holden Capello. My mother is Marie Capello, your ex-wife."

An exasperated sigh bit into the air. "Marie Capello, huh? Why are you calling me?"

"I think you're my father," Holden lobbed into the air where it hung like a cloud enveloped in silence.

"Your father," the man replied, testing the words. "She never told me she was pregnant."

"I just found out about all of this, myself," Holden said tentatively.

An awkward pause filled the air, and Holden was just about to question if Kevin was still on the line when it broke. "I need to think about this. How can I get ahold of you later?"

Holden rattled off his phone number, and Kevin grunted in affirmation.

"Okay, then," Holden said into the awkward silence. "Goodbye."

Kevin paused before answering, but then threw the boy a bone. "Bye, kid."

Holden didn't realize his hands were shaking until he placed his phone on the desk. For better or worse, he'd initiated contact. Now, to wait and see what became of it. He winced a little, knowing that his mother was going to be inherently pissed.

fifteen

MARIE SCROLLED THROUGH HER work emails, trying to decide which emergency required her attention first. She loved the rush and pace of sales, but sometimes she was sick of the "me first" mentality from every single client. "Maybe it's time for a change," she muttered to her coffee cup.

"What's that?" a voice chirped from over the cubicle wall. Marie jumped at the intrusion. She usually enjoyed her weekly day in the office, but today she was not in the mood.

"Nothing, Sally, just talking to myself," Marie answered, then quickly focused her attention to her computer, hoping the visual cue would signal to the head now poking over the divider that she did not want to talk. No luck.

Sally jumped right into her usual never-ending stream of chatter. Marie sighed and turned her body toward Sally to endure a bit of the onslaught. *The poor woman,* Marie thought. *She must be so lonesome.* One of those unique people that required little person-to-person conversation, Marie didn't understand people like Sally who could basically talk to a lamp post as long as it held still. Her good manners required her to nod at the appropriate times as she listened to the latest adventures of Sally's puppy, her son's sports achievements, and her husband's recent motorcycle purchase.

A flood of relief filled her when her phone rang loudly, giving Marie the exit from the conversation that she so desperately needed.

"Sorry, Sally, I'll talk with you later." She smiled, reaching for her phone and thumbing it on before even looking at the display.

"Hello?"

"You horrible bitch," a man's voice seethed into the phone. "You thought you could hide him from me?"

Blood chilled in Marie's veins. For probably the first time in her life, Marie was speechless.

"How long has it been, Marie? Twenty years?"

"Twenty-one. Kevin, I can't talk right now. I'm at work," she said quietly, knowing Sally probably had her ear plastered to the cubicle wall between them.

"I know this is your mobile phone, Marie. I suggest you get to where you *can* talk."

She blew out a big breath. Did she even want to entertain this conversation? Kevin clearly knew about Holden, although she didn't know how. She had to deal with it or let it fester. She steeled her shoulders and made her decision. She hadn't backed down from anything since he hit her that second time. She wasn't going to start now.

"Hold on a minute," she said into the phone. Marie pushed her chair under her desk, grabbed her keys, and made the short walk to the door in record time, nodding politely to coworkers who passed her in the hallway. "I'm here. Why are you calling me?"

A bitter laugh erupted on the other end. "Kind of haughty for someone who's been hiding a big secret for a lot of years, aren't you? Is he mine?"

Marie rolled her eyes. It would be so easy to lie, but Holden already knew the truth. *Surely he didn't contact Kevin…* she thought as her gut twisted. "Yes."

"You didn't think to maybe let me know that I had a kid?" Kevin said coldly.

"I didn't know how long it would take you to sober up enough to even process the information. If you remember, Kevin, you were pretty much continually drunk and useless at that time."

"Sure, throw that back in my face. You're a bitter woman, Marie."

A near-hysterical laugh bubbled from her lips. "Bitter? Yeah, Kevin." She looked around to be sure that nobody was around. "Getting hit by your husband will do that to a woman."

"It was just a little slap," he yelled.

"I'm amazed you even remember!"

It was his turn to laugh. "A person remembers all kinds of things when they wake up and find their wife gone! You cleaned me out, Marie!"

"Are you psychotic? I mean, you are, but are you utterly and completely crazy? We had nothing! You drank all our money! I packed up my clothes and that was it!"

"What about the money?" he hissed.

Marie was stunned into silence.

"Ah! Didn't think I knew about that, did you?"

A sadness fell over Marie where the outrage had been. "Kevin, I had squirreled away five hundred dollars between the first and second time you hit me, just in case it happened again. I knew I'd need gas money to get away."

"Exactly! You stole it!"

"First, it was my money. Second, it's a pathetically small amount. Third, and most disgusting I might add, is the fact that you're missing the point. I had started saving money to use to leave you if you hit me *again*. And you did."

She could hear him breathing heavily into the phone.

"I didn't call to argue with you, you ugly little shrew. I called to let you know that I'm going to make you pay for hiding my son from me."

She closed her eyes and leaned against the brick wall, sick with both dread and relief that this call hadn't come before now. Holden was too smart and good for this crap.

"I'm not going to listen to this. Good luck to you, Kevin."

She clicked off the phone and stayed against the wall until she stopped trembling.

sixteen

A SHIVER SLID DOWN COLE'S BACK as he adjusted his coat collar. Despite the incoming spring, the air still had a serious bite to it. A storm had ravaged the area and branches were down, or partially down, looming dangerously close to the road.

"Forty years on the job, and I still hate this part," Don said, his breath showing in clouds in the air.

"Me too, man. But the quiet is nice," Cole answered with a wry grin.

Don nodded good-naturedly. "Got me there, young man."

Cole picked his way along the path and noted which trees needed to be removed. It was amazing how beautiful and dangerous ice storms could be in the forest.

Systematically, Cole and his crew made their way through the section of the Shawnee National Forest that had been hit hard by an ice storm. Clearing fallen branches didn't top Cole's list of favorite things to do, but it was part of the job.

"Don, what do you think about this one over here," Cole asked, a second before he heard the creak of the tree overhead. He had just enough time to look up and see a huge branch crashing down. *I didn't get to tell Marie how I felt*, he thought with regret as everything went dark.

THE ANTISEPTIC SMELL of the hospital hit Cole's brain before the sound of the monitors pinged into his consciousness. The ache in his head pounded squarely behind his eyes as Cole registered a shape in the chair next to his bed. Levi was definitely not the person he expected to see camped out beside his hospital bed.

"Levi?" Cole rasped, surprised by the sound of his own voice.

"Jesus my all, Cole. You scared us," he answered.

The IV tugged at his wrist as he rubbed his hand along the side of his head. The knot was definitely prominent there.

"One of your guys was just here. Don, I think… He called what hit you a widow-maker."

Cole winced at the term. He'd been around one day when the moniker actually lived up to its name. A huge branch literally fell out of the tree and killed a crew member instantly. The man hadn't stood a chance. He'd never get that scene out of his mind.

"I'm surprised to see you here, Levi. Dancing over my grave, maybe, but not by my bedside."

Levi pulled a face. "I'm under strict orders to bury the hatchet. Turns out Jesse has a low tolerance for b.s., and I've about maxed out my limit for the year." A quiet laugh escaped Cole despite the throb in his head. "Honestly, this weighs on me. I'm not usually one to hold a grudge. And, I'm sorry for what I said at Mallory's party. I dredged up stuff that was your business to share with Marie, not mine," Levi said, raking a hand through his hair. "There's still a piece of me that's inherently pissed that you went after Jesse."

Cole nodded. "I get that. It was low. But, Levi, she's an amazing woman. I had to try."

It was Levi's turn to nod. "I get it. It's hard starting over."

Levi stood and patted Cole hard on the shoulder as Jesse entered the room and pocketed her phone.

"You've done it now," she said to Cole in a sing-song voice.

He half grinned, half grimaced in response. "What now? Jesus, are you this tough on your boys? I'm the one in the hospital bed," he said, pained.

"Yeah. I'm not sure who's more freaked out, your sister or Marie," she said with a wry grin.

"You called Kelly?"

"The hospital did. She was on your next-of-kin paperwork. I just called her with an update, and she'll be here in a few hours. I called Marie, too."

He waited for a beat to see if Marie was on her way. At Jesse's silence, he dragged in a breath. "How did you get pulled into this?" Cole asked, looking from Jesse to Levi, attributing his confusion to more than his apparent concussion.

Jesse was the first to answer. "Ryan was also on your paperwork. He got in touch and let us know you were out here. He would've come himself, but one of his kids has the flu and he didn't want to bring you any more germs." She shrugged and tucked the blanket over his feet.

A sense of sadness flooded over Cole, even though he knew he ought to be thankful to have the scanty support system that he had. At his age, he ought to have a wife and children instead of a sister, neighbor, and awkward ex-girlfriend gathered around his hospital bed. "Thanks for coming, guys. Sorry for the trouble it's been."

"It's not trouble," she answered, shooting a warning look at Levi, just in case. "We're just glad you came out of it so fast. This is all a little weird, Cole... but we were a family when we were younger. We can be a big family again. We're all back home and settled now," she said with a squeeze of Levi's arm. "Face it, we're all thrown together in this little town. It's okay to lean on one another from time to time. You'd be there for us if we needed you, and you know it."

A pit of guilt settled in his stomach, remembering how

he'd retreated from her life when Jesse's dad had died. He ought to have done more than pick a fight with her ex-husband then vanish. "Jesse, I'm sorry I disappeared when your dad died. I was such an idiot."

"There was a lot going on back then, Cole. And I forgive you for being an idiot," she said with a wink as she held his cup and straw to his lips. Cole smirked. Jesse's mothering instinct was so strong, she probably didn't even realize how ridiculous it was for her to try and hold his cup. He took it from her hands and felt his face flush with embarrassment. He had so many mistakes in his past. He'd never make up for all of them. Throwing Marie's son against his own wall ranked pretty high on the chart of things that never should have happened. *No, you already apologized for that. Accept it, she'll never let that go.*

"Look, we've got to head out. Her mom's not available to watch the kids. Michael is trustworthy, but four kids is a little too much, even for him," Levi said. He looked at his watch. "Your sister will be here soon." Levi leaned in closer. "And if I can read *her*," he said, tilting his head toward Jesse, "I expect Marie said she was on her way as well. Might want to do something about that hair." Levi faked a wince as Jesse swatted his arm.

"Take care, Cole. We'll check in tomorrow," Jesse said.

"Thanks for coming, guys."

"Was I right?" Levi asked, draping an arm across Jesse's shoulders as they walked through the parking lot.

Jesse pulled Levi to her side. "Of course. I didn't mean to be out of the room so long. She had a lot to say." She hauled herself into the pick-up truck and waited for Levi to walk around to his own door before continuing. She still couldn't believe he opened her door every time. "I don't know how she manages to say so much, so fast. Her ex was released from prison, but I think we knew about that before she left, right?" She fanned her hand in the air. "Anyway, he found out about Holden."

"Oh no," Levi muttered.

Jesse shook her head and sighed. "I can't believe she made it that long. Apparently, Kevin called Marie at work and threatened to make her pay for hiding Holden from him," Jesse said with a shiver. "It sounds like that guy was a creep before he accidentally killed his second wife. I can't imagine being on the other end of that call."

Levi looked at her like she had two heads. "I know. That sounded terrible, didn't it?" She shrugged. "Still, I mean, it is what it is. He did go to prison for manslaughter. Dang. I wonder if he learned even more bad stuff in prison!" She bugged out her eyes and turned toward him.

Her phone beeped, and she absentmindedly extracted it from her pocket. "Isn't that how it goes in the movies?"

"Beats me." Levi shrugged. "My wife won't let me watch shows like that in bed. They creep her out. She keeps me busy anyway." He chuckled.

"Stop it! Oh, and Marie said that it was Cole's fault that he found out. Turns out the dummy showed up at Marie's a few months ago and slammed her son against a wall or something, thinking he was an overnight guest."

Levi sighed. "He's an idiot."

"Agreed. Marie was already pretty much done with him before that, but that about sealed the deal."

"I would think," Levi answered incredulously.

She shrugged. "I know. Seems cut and dried, but you know it's not always like that. I think they are kind of perfect for one another." She laughed when he squeezed her knee and made a face of mock horror. "Come on! She's hell-bent on being in charge of everything because she's never had anyone to lean on. He's lovingly domineering because he's desperate to find someone to take care of. They could probably work if she'd chill out a little bit and realize she doesn't have to do everything the hardest way possible."

A sarcastic laugh left his lips before he could stop it. Jesse leveled a look at him as they turned onto Poets Pass. "And what does that mean?"

"Sounds a little familiar, is all."

She pulled a face, then looked out the window. "I had my reasons," she said softly.

"I know, baby. If they stand a chance of working, Cole's going to have to get a grip on his Jekyll and Hyde thing."

Jesse nodded. "Definitely. He's a pill. I still think they could work, though."

Levi nodded at her phone as he pulled into their

driveway. "Who texted? One of the kids?" He sighed, wondering what sort of mess they were about to walk into. With five kids between them, there was very little solitude in the homefront.

"Oh yeah, let me see." She squinched up her face to read the text.

"Jess, you're going to have to break down and get glasses," he teased, opening the door of his truck.

"You first, Levi." She groaned. "Oh man. The cat's finally out of the bag!"

"What?"

She hopped out of the truck and met him on his side. "I didn't tell you this because it felt gossipy, but Marie and I found a pregnancy test box at Mallory's house the night the poop hit the fan with you and Cole. Anyway, I've been dying to know what that was all about because it was obvious they were arguing that night. Look," she said, holding the phone where he could see as they walked.

Jesse, who was Anna's OB? Looks like it's my turn to add to the family tree. - Mallory

"Wow, didn't see that one coming. She's a little long in the tooth to be just getting started, isn't she?"

Jesse spun on her heel and glared at her husband. "Women are perfectly capable of having babies in their thirties, Levi."

He threw his hands in the air in a surrender gesture. "Whoa, Jesse! I'm not trying to pick a fight here, it's just that most of the women I know started a bit earlier, is all."

She raked her hair into a bun and blew out a frustrated breath. "Sorry, it's just with everything going on politically these days, that just sounded like a very pig-headed thing to say."

"I know, baby. Down with the patriarchy, and all that." He grabbed her in for a hug and laughed at her rolling eyes. "Seriously, though. What's that going to mean for her and Cade, I wonder? And why did she message you instead of Anna?"

Jesse lifted a shoulder. "We've always been a little closer than the two of them. Maybe because we were closer in age," she said with flared nostrils.

Levi rolled his head back and said, "Don't be mad at me. You could have more babies if you wanted. I didn't mean anything by it."

"Don't even start, Levi. No chance. We'd have to build on, and you know I'm over that construction mess," she said with a laugh as the door swung open to, "Moooom! Michael didn't let me…"

Levi grinned. "Brace yourself."

"We've got this," she said, squaring her shoulders.

seventeen

MARIE'S HEELS CLICKED AGAINST the bleached linoleum hospital floor. An older woman glanced up with a kind smile, so Marie adjusted the scowl on her face. She forgot how polite people were here.

"Hello, can you please direct me to Cole Green's room?"

"Your name, dear?" the elderly woman asked.

"Marie Capello. Jesse Murray called to let me know he'd been injured."

At the mention of Jesse's name, the woman smiled and skimmed a list. "That Jesse sure is a sweet thing. So nice to have her back in town. Did you know she went to school with my son, Hank? Oh, my. I think their birthdays were even in the same week, if I remember right." The woman seemed to be waiting on some kind of confirmation, so Marie just smiled inanely.

After an awkward beat, the woman checked the list again. "Mr. Green is on the second floor, room two hundred one."

"Thank you," Marie answered as she forced herself not to shake her head in response to the little woman. *It's just so different here*, she thought to herself.

Just outside the door, Marie stopped to adjust her purse on her shoulder and ran her hands over her hair. She'd excused herself from the client's meeting as soon as she politely could. She had been working on that contract for months; she couldn't afford to just blow them off after fighting to get the meeting. She drew in a shaky breath and reached to knock on the door when it opened. A tall, blonde goddess pulled on the door and jumped when she saw Marie poised to knock. Bright green eyes flashed at Marie in surprise before a wide smile spread across her face.

"You must be Marie," the woman said, stepping back and holding out her hand in greeting.

Taken aback, Marie quirked an eyebrow at the stranger. She certainly didn't look like a nurse. "Yes, I'm Marie, and you are?" she asked, adding a smile to chip away at the accidental frost in her tone.

The goddess grinned. "I'm Kelly, Cole's sister."

Marie felt the ice in her veins thaw a bit when it hit her. "Kelly? So..."

She nodded. "Yes, Kelly Green." She rolled her eyes.

"My mom thought she was so clever. That was her favorite color. It's no wonder I married the first man who asked me. He was a loser, but at least I got rid of that name."

A snort erupted from Marie, proof that the stress of the last few hours had done a number on her. She didn't typically snort at strangers. She let out a big breath. "Nice to meet you, Kelly. Is he…?"

Kelly nodded her head and made a gesture to shoo Marie outside of the room. Marie allowed herself to be shephereded but snuck a peek at the bed. Cole looked like he was spilling out of the edges of the bed at an angle. An IV was attached to his arm, but the rest of him was monitor-free. That had to be a good sign, she thought.

"He just went to sleep, so the nurse asked me to keep it down. I've been here a little over an hour so far, and he's been fighting rest. I hope you don't mind if we wait outside for a bit. Cole's stubborn as a mule, and I'm afraid they're going to have to shoot him with an elephant tranquilizer if he doesn't get some sleep."

Kelly shared Cole's melodious Tennessee accent. Marie could listen to that drawl for days. Maybe she should look at relocating to Tennessee after Holden got out of college. They found the waiting area, and Marie settled in a chair as Kelly grabbed a cup of coffee from the vending machine in the corner.

"I'm sure this is glorious," she said with a precautionary sniff.

"Sure to put hair on your chest, I bet," Marie said with a smile. "My dad used to always say that."

Kelly gave a sympathetic smile. "It's nice to meet you. I heard all about you when you were visiting."

Butterflies took flight in Marie's stomach. Her expression betrayed her thoughts because Kelly gave a small laugh. "Well, not everything. Just the highlights. You were everything—and then, gone."

Not even close to being ready to dish, Marie sidestepped the conversation. "Kelly, my friend Jesse called to let me know Cole had been in an accident, but she didn't have a lot of details about what happened. Do you know?"

She nodded and took a deep breath. "Cole's boss called while I was driving. I just got here a little before you did. Cole and his crew were clearing some felled trees alongside the highway. One took him by surprise, and a friend knocked him out of the way."

"Somebody was big enough to knock Cole out of the way?" Marie asked with huge eyes.

A slight laugh escaped Kelly. "Yeah. Apparently so. Don, the friend, is in his sixties, by the way. He nearly managed to push Cole clear. Cole has a gash on his head and a concussion, and Don got a broken arm for his trouble, but they're both lucky that's all it was."

"Do they know how long he'll be here?" she asked, already wondering who would take care of him all alone on that mountain.

"He'll be here for twenty-four hours for observation and bloodwork," Kelly answered, then chuckled. "The nurse said they knew he had a concussion when they asked who was president and he answered Clinton."

"Oh my," Marie muttered.

Kelly smiled. "He's already cleared up a little since then. They said that was common after a head injury. They'll draw blood every few hours and continue checking him, then he'll be free to go home. I was able to get some time off work so that I can stare at him for a few days, just to be sure he's okay."

Marie visibly relaxed at that news and rubbed her temple and the spot between her eyes hoping to relieve the headache building there. She cringed as tears filled her eyes. She wasn't a crier, and she definitely didn't want to cry in front of Cole's sister. *I should be supporting Kelly right now, not the other way around. His sister, for Pete's sake! Who even is Cole to me? Some fling? A good vacation memory? Why am I still thinking about this man?*

The quiet tears turned to sobs, and Marie put her hands over her eyes. "I'm sorry, Kelly, this is so stupid."

She looked up to see wet, green eyes half-smiling at her. "It's okay to cry, Marie. This is scary. Cole could've been killed today." A sob worked its way up her throat, and the women embraced in a hug. A few minutes ticked by, and they were dabbing eyes with tissues as a nurse came to their area.

"Kelly, your brother is awake now," the nurse said with a tap to her shoulder. "You can go back in if you'd like."

"Actually, I'll give Marie some time. I'm sure Cole would like to see her," she said with a small smile.

Marie nodded in thanks and ran her hands over her hair

as she walked to the room. At the door, she drew in a deep breath, willing herself to maintain her composure. Releasing it, she walked in.

Cole opened groggy eyes at the sound of footsteps. Marie watched as his eyes opened wide at the sight of her.

"Marie," he said, breathing her name like a prayer.

She forced a smile to her lips even though smiling was the last thing she felt like doing as she took in the cut marring the side of his head and corner of his temple. Marie sat lightly on the small amount of space he wasn't using on the hospital bed and raised a hand to his face. "Cole, I'm so—" she paused, her eyes closing briefly as she willed the quiver from her voice. "I'm so glad you're still... here," Marie said lamely.

Cole's hand covered hers, and he gave it a squeeze. "Me, too. Marie, I'm so sorry. I'm so sorry that I freaked out and put your son up against the wall. I'm so sorry for so much that I've done," he said, as his hand moved from hers to the bed. Sheets twisted in his hands as his rumbling baritone softly filled the room. "Basically, Marie, I'm a screw up. I try to keep it together." He raised his eyes to hers. "I do. When someone messes with someone I love, it just goes right through me."

He continued speaking, but Marie didn't hear anything after he uttered the word "love." Her head swam as his words reverberated around her skull like a marble in a Mason jar. "I'm sorry, *love?*" she blurted in the middle of his confession.

"What?" Cole said, confusion written all over his face.

She took and released a breath slowly. "You said, 'when someone messes with someone I love,'" Marie posed, unsure.

Cole raised a shoulder. "Yeah," he answered cautiously.

Marie stood, placing her hand on his wrist. "Cole, love is something more than a feeling. Love is waking up at three AM to strip puke-filled sheets when your kid makes a mess. It's working to make everything 'all better' when there is no freaking *all better*. It's waking up alone night after night so that your baby doesn't have to suffer any confusion about what is stable and what is not. It's putting yourself on hold year after year with zero regret or hesitation.

"Love isn't the happy feeling you get when you wonder what another person is doing in the middle of their day. It's not hearing a song on the radio and thinking to yourself that that person would truly enjoy that song. It's not eating a meal that rings all your bells and stopping to think how much that person would enjoy the flavor. It's nothing like that! Love is sacrifice and heartache and a feeling of doing without for the sake of the greater good!" she railed, cursing her trembling voice up one side and down the other.

Somehow, Cole pulled Marie back down to his side and flinched as the machine alarm sounded when his heart rate got above the recommended range for someone in his condition. He forced a few slow, deep breaths and got himself under control before a nurse came to check on him. "Marie, listen to me. Love isn't supposed to be all about sacrifice and going it alone. It's being there for each other. It's standing up when the other feels weak. I'll do that for you, Marie, if you'll just have me," Cole said, tears welling in his eyes.

She shook her head as the words spilled from his lips. "I can't deal with that, Cole. It's opening myself up for disaster," she said, David's article flashing before her eyes. She'd never forget the feeling of humiliation when she picked up that paper and saw that her only serious boyfriend of the last two decades had blasted monogamy. Marie shook her head to clear away that image as her stomach twisted in knots. "Listen, Cole, it's been Holden and me for a hundred years, and I can't let anyone else in because," she said, her voice catching, "because, what if you tear me apart?" Her final words were barely a whisper.

"Tear you apart, Marie?" Cole replied, grabbing at her hands. "That's not what love does!"

She shook her head at him and withdrew her hands from his. "You don't know yet, Cole. It's not all promises, back rubs, and uninterrupted sex. It's exhaustion. It's ailing parents. It's illness. It's also awesome days filled with successful workdays, happy phone calls from self-sufficient kids, and even a pleasant sort of boredom and routine. It's fifteen good days, and then all of a sudden your ex is on the phone telling you how he's going to tell your baby what a lying piece of trash you are that you kept him from his own father. Then, every time the phone rings, you flinch and feel afraid to answer. Then, you feel ashamed of yourself for letting anyone make you feel afraid ever again!" she said in a rush, up and pacing around the little room.

"Wait a minute," he asked, gingerly pushing himself into a sitting position in the hospital bed. "Your ex has been threatening you?"

Marie paced to the corner of the room and wiped at the traitorous tears that slipped down her face in double time.

"It's nothing. Holden is too smart for any of Kevin's idiocy," she said, cockily raising a shoulder. "He gets it from me." She smirked, wiping her face. "But it gets old, you know?" she winced, prickling with unease as Cole reached out to her when she passed close to the bed

"Screw it," he murmured, pulling the IV from his arm and embracing Marie in his strong arms.

She had exactly thirty seconds to melt into him until an elderly nurse bustled into his room to silence the blaring monitor. "Mr. Green, you're going to have to at least *attempt* to keep this in your arm unless you want to get a god-awful infection that could cost you your limb," she blustered, swatting in Marie's direction as she scampered off the narrow bed.

"I'm sorry, ma'am," he muttered in his sincere Southern drawl.

Marie peeked at him from the corner of the cramped room as the nurse reinserted Cole's IV. She watched his face as the needle hit home, seeing him flinch a tiny bit.

So he is mortal, she said to herself, not having been convinced before then that Cole was, in fact, a normal human. After the nurse bustled from the room, Marie settled on the bed once more. Her hand instinctively rested on his knee.

"When did this all start, Marie? When did he start bothering you?"

Her shoulder lifted slightly. "You sure you want me to answer that?" she asked, her eyes crinkled in a wince.

Cole closed his eyes and exhaled, guilt finding its familiar weight in his chest. "What happened?"

He watched her shoulders rise and fall before she spoke. "The day you popped in for a visit and scared the bejesus out of my son," she said with a pause, "he overhead us talking about Kevin. It wasn't long before I got a call at work that Kevin had found out about Holden. He got in touch with him somehow, but he won't talk to me about it."

Regret hit him like a sledgehammer. "Marie," he whispered as he laid his head on the pillow and stared at the ceiling. The rest of his sentence didn't come; there weren't words to be said. She sat there in silence, holding his hand in hers.

"How old is he again? How many years did you manage to keep Holden from this asshole before I came on the scene and literally ruined everything?" Cole asked with steel filling his voice.

Marie turned her shoulders and answered gently, "Twenty-one. I can't believe how fast time goes. My parents always said once he entered kindergarten that it would fly, and it did. We've been so lucky that Kevin didn't find out about him earlier." She tilted her head to the ceiling and pulled her hands to her neck to rub at the clenched muscles there. "I can't imagine if I'd had to share Holden as a child with that idiot. Can you imagine me hauling my son into a prison to visit his father? How might that have changed Holden?"

Cole's hands replaced her own on her neck and she, the walking iceberg that she was, melted by half an inch. "I know what you're saying, but it's a reality for a lot of kids, Marie. That doesn't mean the cycle perpetuates. It would be a scary thing to have to do, though."

For a second, his words felt like a contradiction, and she bristled. When she turned to look at him, she saw something in his eyes that he clearly wasn't planning to share. Marie tried to envision a little Cole and Kelly being trotted into a prison visitor's lobby to see their father. She'd stuck her foot in her mouth once again.

She wasn't sure what to say next, so she just waited and recognized the silence wasn't as uncomfortable as she thought it would have been, given their time apart. Her eyes raked over this gloriously complicated man and a smirk touched her lips. It didn't go unnoticed.

Cole self-consciously touched his bandaged and banged up head. "What's that about?" he asked her sheepishly.

She started to speak, but caught the bashful look on his face and felt her cheeks heat up. A laugh bubbled up from her belly and erupted from her lips. His brows drew together in confusion, which didn't do anything but make Marie get more tickled. Tears started to stream, and then she snorted, wiping frantically at her eyes.

"Oh my gosh, I'm sorry," she said, wrinkling her nose

in embarrassment. "What are the freaking odds of..." she gestured between them back and forth, "whatever this is. I mean, I get stuck out in the country, and you roll up like some kind of white knight, except you're also kind of, I don't know, whatever the opposite of a white knight is. We have mind-blowing sex, I find out you've had a fling with my dear friend, and then you spill the biggest secret of my life."

Cole cringed at the partial histeria in her voice.

"I don't know whether to jump your bones or run you over with my car! God bless America," she said, then bent over putting her head between her knees to breathe deeply.

He rubbed his hand on her back in a comforting circle. "I get that a lot." He grinned when her head shot up in surprise.

eighteen

"WELL, HOW DID YOU LEAVE IT?" Jesse asked Marie as they settled into a booth at the Mountaintop Bar and Grille. Her phone dinged and she read a text. "Mallory and Anna will be here any minute. Apparently Anna's taking forever to say goodbye to Benji," Jesse said, a grin automatically forming on her face.

"He's a cutie, huh?" Marie asked.

"The cutest. He's so pleasant and sleeps really well already. Figures."

"Jesse! That's not very nice!"

"I know, but all three of my boys were terrible sleepers. How unfair is that?" she asked, throwing her hands up in exasperation. "Two orders of cheese curds, one water, and three tall beers, please. There are two more joining us. They're not all for me or anything," Jesse amended to the waitress.

Marie rolled her eyes and whispered when the cute little twenty-something walked back to the kitchen, stopping to check her phone halfway through the restaurant. "Are you seriously defending your order to the waitress?"

"Hey man, it's a small town," she answered. Seeing that did not mean anything to Marie, she added, "Give me a break. I live here, Marie. People love to gossip! Anyway, how did you leave it with Cole?" Jesse asked, then smiled and stood as Mallory and Anna bustled through the door.

Greetings and hugs were shared, and moans of relief were made when the waitress brought out Jesse's order.

"Ah, beer!" Anna said and chugged half of hers. "Man, I haven't had a beer in ages," she smiled down to her toes as she wiped her mouth with her napkin.

"Pump and dump?" Jesse asked.

"First ever." Anna grinned.

"Good Lord!" Mallory exclaimed to Anna. "Are those things for real?" she asked, not even trying to disguise her shock at Anna's sizable chest.

Anna blushed from her scalp to the soles of her feet and rolled her eyes at Mallory. "Are you serious right now?"

"How did I not see those things before? You've never had any boobs, Anna. Oh my gosh. I'm doomed," she said, looking down at her own big boobs.

Marie's head jerked from Mallory to Jesse and back.

Jesse nodded. "Cat's out of the bag now, I guess. We can probably confess," Jesse whispered conspiratorially.

"To what?" Mallory asked.

"We saw the pregnancy test box the night of your house-warming party," Jesse admitted.

Mallory groaned, and Anna made a face of disgust.

"Good grief. What were you doing, rooting through her trash, Jesse? You can't take her anywhere without her peeking in medicine cabinets and closets," Anna informed Mallory and Marie.

"Now you tell me," Mallory sighed. "Anyway, yeah. That was the night it all hit the fan."

"What happened?" Jesse asked in true nosey fashion. "I don't know him well, but Cade seemed to be in rare form that night."

"Yeah, he and I got into it. I had been feeling off and took a test. Well, you know that, apparently," she said with a quirk of her eye brow. "Anyway, Cade found the pregnancy test box before I had mentioned anything about wondering if I was pregnant. He got all bent out of shape that I didn't tell him earlier."

Anna snorted beside her. Mallory shot her a look, and she threw her hand up in defense. "I'm not laughing at you! I swear. He thinks that's bad? He'd have died if he knew what happened with me and Aidan. I was a few months pregnant before Aidan knew. He didn't take it well at all."

"At all!" Jesse emphasized. "Anyway, what did he say?"

"I don't remember all of it, but the most surprising part was when he proposed that night."

"*What?*" Anna and Jesse said in unison.

"Yeah, right there. Right after he tried to admonish me for not telling him about my suspicion. Then, he got super upset when I told him I needed more time to think about it. We'd only been together a few months at that point. What?" she said to Jesse's bemused face.

"Nothing." She shrugged.

"What?" Mallory pressed.

Jesse leaned back in her chair and grinned. "I tell ya, there's something magical about this place."

Mallory looked around the restaurant, confused.

"No, dummy. Not this restaurant. This place..." she gestured around, "home. I found Levi again after all these years." She pointed to her sister. "You rekindled things with Aidan—with a *bang*," she joked, flaring her fingers out in exaggerated jazz hands, sending Anna into a fit of laughter. She turned to Mallory. "And you... you've managed to tame the untamable, if what Avery's shared about Cade is true. And you're just as bad as he is."

"Hey," Mallory whined.

"You know what I mean. Neither one of you have ever been engaged, right? Yet he proposed, and your answer was?"

Mallory shrugged, but a small grin tugged at the corner of her lips. "I'm thinking about it."

The ladies all smiled back at her as Jesse continued. "Now, the question is, what are we going to do with you?" she said, turning toward Marie with her hand fisted under her chin in contemplation as she leaned against the tabletop.

Marie shook her head. "No way. Leave me out of this."

"Come on now, spill. How did you leave things with Cole when you left the hospital?" The other ladies were glued to her every word.

"Kind of with a fit of hysteria, but not in a bad way," she answered truthfully.

"Marie," Jesse scolded. "Did you yell at a man with a concussion? In a hospital, no less?"

"Oh Lord." Mallory sighed.

"That's her Mom voice," Anna whispered to Mallory, who nodded in reply.

Marie gave Jesse the stink-eye. "Not really. I just told him I need time and space to think about what to do." She bit a corner of her lip and looked down at the table. "I told him that I'd call him."

"Oohh," Anna said.

"Yeah. That sort of makes me a jerk, I guess," Marie said, looking up at Jesse. "But, the ball is in my court."

"Right where you like it," Jesse said quietly.

"Pot, meet Kettle," Anna said in a sing-song voice and stuck her tongue out in return to her sister's glare.

"Yeah, yeah. I'm not going to lie, you guys. I'm more attracted to him than I've been with any man my whole life. Way more. Way more than David," she added.

"David was a douche," Jesse added.

"The worst kind of douche," Marie agreed.

Anna chimed in, "What's the hold up?"

"He's a little…" she paused, trying to find the right word. "Unhinged?" she asked, looking to Jesse for confirmation.

"Unhinged? Sounds like I'm needed here," a voice called out from behind Marie's back. A gorgeous blonde with a bob smiled down at her. "I'm Avery."

"She's a shrink," Anna offered helpfully.

"Nice to meet you," Marie said, reaching out to shake the offered hand.

Avery pulled a chair up to the end of the table and glanced around. "What are we drinking tonight?" she asked, raising her hand to flag the attention of a waitress.

"All beer, except for her. Only water for her," Jesse said with a nod toward Mallory.

Avery's eyes lit up. "Water for you, huh? Congratulations!"

"What? I could just be giving up beer!" Mallory teased.

"You? Never," Avery answered.

"You're right, and thank you," she said, returning Avery's quick hug.

"Do I know before Jake?" Avery asked, an evil grin plastered to her face.

"Yes, and don't you dare tell him. I'm going to tell him this weekend," Mallory threatened.

Avery made a scout's honor gesture as she ordered her beverage. "You've got it, Mal. So, what were you talking about? Who's unhinged?"

Marie sighed heavily. "My sex god."

"I always miss the good parts of the conversations," Avery whined.

Jesse looked at Marie and silently asked for permission to spill the beans. At Marie's nod, she launched in and summarized what they'd covered for Avery.

"Yikes," Avery answered after getting the rundown. "He doesn't really sound unhinged… but definitely aggressive."

Jesse kind of waggled her head in indecision. "His heart's in the right place, though."

"Yeah, unlike this piece of work," Marie said, pulling her phone from her pocket.

"What's going on?" Mallory leaned in, trying to see what Marie was showing Jesse.

"My ex-husband. My convict ex-husband. Wait. My *murdering* ex-husband," Marie said, tossing the phone on the table.

Sounds of shock came from Avery, Anna, and Mallory. "He was convicted of manslaughter for indirectly causing the death of his next wife. We weren't together long. He hit me a few times, and I bailed. He remarried, hit her, and she struck her head and died. He just got out of prison and found out about my son, well *our* son, Holden.

"Holden's hacked that I lied to him about not knowing who his father was. I didn't know I was pregnant when I divorced Kevin. I certainly didn't want to drag him in and out of prison throughout his childhood to visit his father, so I just left that part out. Not the honest approach, but I wouldn't do it any differently."

The ladies nodded in agreement, and Marie continued, "Anyway, Holden reached out to Kevin like the stubborn arse he can be, and now Kevin is determined to get me back for withholding his child from him all of these years. He keeps calling and hanging up at all hours. I'm tempted to block him, but I'm afraid something will happen and I'll need his number, now that Holden is in touch with him." She sighed and scrubbed her hand against her forehead.

"Holden told me last night that he plans to meet Kevin for dinner soon. He doesn't want me there. I just told him to be sure it's in a public place and not to trust Kevin any farther than he could throw him. He's going to meet him whether or not I consent. He's twenty-one, for Pete's sake. The best I can do is caution him. What hacks me off..."

"Despite the lack of control," Jesse supplied.

"Absolutely *that*, but what gets me even more than that is how defensive Holden gets every time I warn him about meeting in public, or not riding in Kevin's car—if he even has one—or not giving any personal information, or money, for God's sake. Can you imagine?" she rambled and shook her head.

Mallory took a drink of her water and looked longingly at Jesse's beer before responding. "Does he feel like you're smothering him?"

Marie shot her a look. "Maybe."

Mallory rebuffed the pointed look from Jesse. "What? That's how I'd feel if my mom told me all that stuff at twenty-one."

Anna chuckled. "Huh? Aunt Ruthie can be a smother-mother?"

Mallory laughed and bugged out her eyes. "Yeah, just a little bit."

Avery cackled at Mallory's comment, and then turned big eyes on Mallory. "What? I'm not saying a word!"

Anna leaned forward. "Didn't she practically force you to sleep over at her house when your house was broken into?"

At Avery's nod, she added, "Isn't that when you and Jake hooked up the first time? Right under that poor woman's own roof." She clucked in disapproval as Avery choked on her sip of beer.

Jesse leaned in. "What? The horror!" she exclaimed in mock disbelief.

Marie frantically grabbed napkins to pass to Avery to dab at her beer-covered silk blouse.

"Oh my Lord," Avery muttered. "We did not hook up... that night," she added with a grin.

The women cackled as the waitress came by offering a second round. At Jesse's nod, she returned back to the bar. Marie looked around at her tablemates like they were crazy. They flitted from conversation to conversation like butterflies in a flower garden.

"Anyway, Marie, maybe Holden thinks you're mothering him too much. He's a big, bad twenty-one-year-old, used to calling his own shots, right? He doesn't live at home, does he?"

Marie bugged out her eyes. "Absolutely not! He's finishing up his last year in college and lives in an apartment near campus. I'd let him live at home if he wanted, though. Hell, I'd let him live with me forever. He's been my buddy for a long time. He's practically perfect," she said with a smile.

"Oh Lord, his wife's going to hate you," Anna said, laughing at Marie's extended middle finger. "I like her, Jess, can we keep her?"

Jesse smiled and nodded. "I hope so."

Marie rolled her eyes and took another sip of her beer. She could get used to having a little clutch of girlfriends to get together with.

Your life's in St. Louis, her brain reminded her. *Shhh! Let me just enjoy this. Just for a little while longer.*

nineteen

"So why can't you just move down there, Marie?" Dr. Klein asked bluntly.

"Did you not hear anything I just said?" she asked, exasperated.

Dr. Klein tapped his chin with his pen in his equally endearing and annoying habit. "Well, I heard you say that you like it down there. That you felt more at peace there than you've felt here in years. That you have a group of friends that you enjoy spending time with. Also, I heard you say that you could technically do your job from anywhere with a decent internet connection and highway access. Did I get that right?" he asked in response to her sour expression.

"What about the crazy caveman part?" she asked, standing and beginning to pace in front of his windows.

"Why does moving down there have to do anything with him, if you're uncertain of your feelings for, uh, Cole, was it?"

She sighed. "Yes, Cole. I mean, it doesn't necessarily have anything to do with him. It's just that he'll be closer if I'm down there."

He wrinkled his brow at her. "So?"

"So," she repeated, and flopped ungraciously back in her seat. "So, if he's close to me I'm going to do something stupid like marry him."

Dr. Klein smiled. "Ah, yes, I see how that could be tragic. You might marry someone who wants you back, who seems to provide for himself well, and according to what else you shared, uh, let me find it here, and I quote, 'Absolutely curls my toes.'"

"I did not say that!" Marie said, scurrying to his chair where he was pointing with his pen. "I did. I did say that."

She sat down again and put her head in her hands. "But he's irrational. He's emotional. He's... he's... he's... unpredictable!"

"Since when does everything have to be predictable, Marie?"

She lifted her shoulders in response. "He's aggressive."

Dr. Klein uncrossed his legs and leaned forward toward her. "*You're* aggressive," he said quietly. "It's not always just opposites that attract, Marie. Plus, I'm not telling you to marry the guy. I'm just telling you to consider something with one positive green flag after another. All signs point to 'go.'"

She didn't respond, so he continued. "You have been a free agent for as long as I've known you. You've raised an awesome kid who is well-rounded and independent. You are successful in your career. You've got the nicest shoe and purse collection I've ever seen," Dr. Klein said with a laugh.

Marie smiled as her therapist laughed in his funny way, shoulders rising and falling with each laugh. He was quirky, but fantastic at his job.

"Look, don't let your fear of change—or of giving up control—stop you from making a change that might end up bringing you a lot of joy. I mean that with Cole in or out of the picture. Maybe you stay by yourself forever and continue to call all the shots. Or, maybe you trust your heart to love again."

"And potentially get stomped again."

The doctor shrugged. "Or, get stomped again. That's always a chance we take when we love."

Marie's eyes lingered on the wedding ring Dr. Klein absentmindedly spun on his finger. His wife had passed away nearly a year ago from a long-term illness. A whole year later he still wore the ring, and Marie imagined he always would.

"I'm your therapist. Your sounding board. I'd be happy to have you stay right here and continue to come see me, and watch you as you continue to sort more and more out on your own. I get attached to patients after being in their lives for so long. I enjoy watching my patients take control over things that used to unravel them. I like seeing you here, stronger than you've been since the whole David fiasco. But, I'd be even happier knowing you were on a path that serves you to the highest level. You have to do the hard work of figuring what that path is, though. I can't do that part."

Marie nodded and walked over to Dr. Klein. He stood after glancing at the clock to see their time was already over.

"See you next time," Marie said, reaching over to give the gentle doctor's hand a squeeze.

"See you later, Marie. Take care," he said with a smile, readjusting his glasses on the top of his head before returning to his desk to file away her folder.

twenty

"I CAN'T BELIEVE THIS," Holden hissed, wiping his palms on his jeans for the tenth time in thirty minutes. He felt ashamed to be so nervous as he waited at the cafe for his father to show up. He glanced at his watch again, noting that Kevin was already ten minutes late. "Five more minutes," he said aloud to no one.

As the clock reached the fifth minute, he stood and pulled the ball cap from his head, swiping his hair back before resettling the cap on his head. "This is ridiculous," he said quietly and went to push in his chair. He turned to the door and saw someone walking in. His heart leapt to his throat as he watched an older version of himself walk toward the table.

The man didn't break eye contact as he crossed the small cafe, but he didn't smile either. Kevin stopped a few feet away and stared. Holden didn't know whether to say hello or tell the dude that he was late. His upbringing got the best of him, and he stood and offered his hand to the man. "I was just about to leave; glad you could make it."

Kevin took his hand in a firm handshake and gave a smile that Holden thought didn't quite reach his eyes.

"You've got her hair, huh?" Kevin asked, a grim look on his face.

Holden pulled the cap off, revealing glossy, black curls. "Yes, sir," he said with a self-effacing grin. "I hated it when I was little, until I got to high school and found out that girls dig curls."

"Girls dig curls," Kevin repeated, shaking his head. "If you say so, kid. Sorry I was late. Don't have a car yet. What do you drive?" Kevin asked, turning to scan the parking lot.

Somewhere in the back of his mind Holden heard his mother and her relentless warnings about not giving too much information away. The look in Kevin's eyes triggered some kind of unease in Holden, so he did something he never did. He lied.

"I had a buddy drop me off today. He'll be back in a while," Holden lied, quickly changing the subject. "So, I don't know anything about you," he said, instantly regretting his word choice at the flinch on Kevin's face. It wasn't like he could ask him where he lived, because he surely wasn't going to answer. He couldn't ask about where he'd been living—

he'd been in prison for heaven's sake. Conversation topics were a little limited.

A bitter laugh escaped Kevin before answering. "Yeah, man, that wasn't exactly my doing." He turned his bright blue eyes on Holden. "What to tell you…" he said, his voice trailing off. "Well, I guess I could tell you about your grandparents, now that you know they once existed," he scoffed.

Holden gave a sort of smile, uncertain how to respond to the blatant animosity. He was ticked at his mother for not being honest with him, but he wasn't going to listen to this man, the man that hit her, talk ugly about her. Kevin began talking about where his parents had lived and worked, and that he had a brother that lived in New Jersey. Holden's attention wavered as the man talked. His mind kept going back to how Marie said that Kevin had hit her a few times. He wanted to hate Kevin, but he wanted to be around him long enough to learn more about him. He was his father, after all, but a sense of guilt wedged uncomfortably in his belly at the fact he wanted to know Kevin at all.

His attention refocused in time to listen to the medical history Kevin was sharing. At least that was something he actually needed to know. Thankfully, though they sounded meaner than striped snakes, his father's people had been relatively healthy, with the exception of his grandfather who died from lung cancer. The conversation ended awkwardly, and Kevin pulled his phone out to check the time.

"Well, kid, this has been interesting," he said with a sort of smile. "You don't talk much, do you?"

"Eh, this is kind of new to me here," Holden answered, stopping himself as he started to pull the keys from his pocket.

"Yeah, same here. I'm not real good at this," he said, leaving Holden to wonder if he meant talking to his son, or talking period. "I got someplace to be here in a bit, so I'm going to get started walking. Take care," he said, landing a big clap to Holden's back.

Holden thought instantly of what that strong hand would feel like striking him in the face, and his guts turned to water. He masked his reaction and managed a smile. "I'll be in touch soon," he lied.

Kevin leaned in, and Holden got a whiff of the stale scent of cigarettes. "Oh, don't worry. I'll see you again real soon," he said as he tossed a wrinkled twenty-dollar bill on the table, more than covering the quick lunch.

As soon as Kevin hit the door, Holden headed to the bathroom where he puked up the remnants of the cheeseburger he'd choked down while Kevin talked. He was not looking forward to rehashing this with his mother. He hated when she was right. *She was always right,* he thought to himself.

twenty-one

MARIE CHECKED HER PHONE for what had to be the fifth time in an hour. Holden still hadn't responded to let her know if he was coming home this weekend. He was usually pretty good about answering her messages and calls. She still hadn't heard from Cole, either, however she was the one that said she'd call him. There was one person she knew would always answer the phone.

"Hello?" the sweet voice answered.

"Hi, Mom, how are you?" Marie asked, then set to cleaning her kitchen. When she talked to her mom, she could always count on a full recap of the day's activities, conversations, and even meals. Marie smiled absentmindedly as she listened to her mother's voice. She was so thankful that her mother was still healthy.

When she realized her mother had paused, she replayed the last sentence that she'd heard. "Yes, Mom. Holden's doing well. I'm still waiting to find out if he's coming in this weekend. Would you like to go to lunch if he does? I can pick you up."

While her mother debated which restaurant they should visit and which art exhibit she'd most like to see, Marie weighed dropping the bomb on her mother and decided to go for it.

"Mom," she said, taking a quick breath. "There's some new stuff going on in my life, and I want to run both by you and get your advice."

Instant panic filled her mother's voice. "What is it, Marie?" She could completely envision her mother's spine going rigid and her blue eyes widening.

She gestured that everything was okay, even though she was alone in her kitchen alone rather than face to face. "It's fine, I mean, it's going to be fine, it's just..." her voice trailed off and she heaved a big sigh. "I'll just spit it out. I'm considering moving, and want to know if you'll come with me."

"Oh holy hell, Marie. You scared the crap out of me. Of course, I'll move. Where are we going?" she asked with near exasperation.

A laugh bubbled out of Marie before she could catch herself. She perched on the counter and stared up at the popcorn ceiling that she'd never liked. "Well, that was easier than I thought it would be."

"I'm game. Where are we going? Someplace beachy?" her mother asked, a smile in her voice.

Marie winced. "Well, not exactly. How about the middle of nowhere."

"What are you talking about, Marie?"

Marie hopped down from her perch on the counter and began to slowly walk circles around her kitchen island. "Well, remember that little cabin I rented a few months back?"

"Oh, no, Marie. I won't live in the woods, honey. I'm too old."

Her head shook in answer. "No, Mom. I don't want us to live in the woods. There's a neat little town nearby. I can't believe I'm saying this, but I loved it there. I'd have friends there—"

Her mother interrupted her, something that happened more and more as of late. "Friends? That would be a nice change for you, dear."

Marie ignored the unintentional jab. "Yes, it would. And, well, I probably should've told you earlier, but I met someone while I was down there."

"Now, I can see moving somewhere because you liked the town and have friends there, but I'm not sure you want to relocate because of some man. I mean, especially one you didn't tell your mother about," her mother warned.

She inhaled and rubbed that spot between her eyes that looked like a permanent wrinkle when she was frustrated. "Not just for him, Mom, but he'd be a nice perk."

"Hmm. Well, do they have retirement villages down there like I have here? No offense, Marie, but we'd kill each other if we lived together."

Marie agreed wholeheartedly. "Yes, Mom. I already did some checking, and the cost will be the same and they take your insurance," she said, heading off what would surely be the next question.

"Send me the name, and I'll Google it," her mother answered, causing Marie to smile. Her mother was a ninja when it came to Googling.

"I will, Mom. I'm glad to hear you're game. Something else has come up."

"Well, it'll have to be a whopper to top this!" her mother hooted. "Shoot."

"Holden found out about Kevin, and they've been getting together to visit," she blurted.

A low whistle reverberated in the phone. "I did not expect that one. I thought you were going to say you got fired or something," her mother answered.

Marie frowned at the phone, then put it back to her ear. "No, Mom, work is still going well, thank goodness," she said, not even wanting to contemplate what she'd do if that crapped out.

"So, how's Holden doing? What's Kevin like now?" she asked. Then she grumbled, "I don't imagine prison improved him."

"That's the thing," she said slowly. "I haven't seen him; Holden's met him on his own."

"Oh, Marie. I don't like this. I don't like this at all!"

A heavy sigh left Marie. "I don't like it either. It sounds like the first meeting was rough, but afterward, Kevin warmed up a little. So far it's been halfway between the city and where Holden lives. I warned him not to share any personal information. Who knows what he's saying, though. He always assumes the best of people."

"He does. The boy is totally green."

Marie grinned. "He is. He's unsuspecting. That's what freaks me out the most."

"Well, dear, any more big news, or is that about it?" her mother asked.

Marie eyeballed the clock and smiled. "Card game?"

"Yeah, the ladies' poker game starts in about twenty minutes, and I have to walk down to the ballroom and get set up."

"No, nothing else to add, thank God," Marie answered.

"Don't forget to send me the name of that place, and I'll check it out. And send me that man's name, too. I'll Google him, make sure he's okay for you. Let me know if Holden is coming in, otherwise I might go to the Botanical Gardens instead of lunch. They're renting us a bus!" her mother said excitedly.

"Okay, Mom. Love you."

"Love you, too, Marie. Bye bye," her mother said, then disconnected the call.

twenty-two

A BLACK LAB RACED AROUND TO Cole's back porch as he sat looking out over the firepit.

"Easy, fella, where'd you come from?" Cole asked, scooping up the little butterball. Dodging licks, he heard footsteps and turned to face whoever was coming around the corner.

"Blue? Blue!" Cole heard a man yelling in his yard.

Ryan surfaced and shook his head as he made his way to the deck. "I caved, man. I couldn't take it any longer."

Cole crooked an eyebrow at his friend. "The wife or the kids?"

"All of them. They turned on me. Who do you think takes this little turd outside at night when it's scary, raining, or five AM?" Ryan asked. "Me. That's who."

"Scary? You grew up in these woods, man. You can't just let him outside?" Cole asked, snuggling the puppy into his lap as he sat back down in the chair.

"No way. My luck something would gobble him up. Won't be long, though. Look how big his paws are. He's going to be a monster."

Cole nodded and continued looking the puppy over. "Blue, huh?"

"Yeah, I made them a deal. They could pick out the puppy, but I wanted to name him." Ryan grinned.

"Why Blue?"

"'Cause I always wanted a Blue Heeler."

Cole looked confused. "This is a Lab, man."

"Yeah, but he doesn't know that," Ryan answered. "Hey, who was at your house yesterday? They about nailed me when I crossed the road on the 4-wheeler."

"Out checking fences?" Cole asked.

"Yeah. Had some down, and one of the god-dang mules got out and trotted right up to the kitchen door. Amy almost gave up the ghost when she saw that," he said with a chuckle.

"Had an appraiser out to check out the place," Cole said, dreading the next question.

Ryan's eyebrows raised to the sky. Shockingly he was silent an entire minute before speaking again. "You're not leaving, are you, Cole?"

He lifted a shoulder in response. "Checking out my options."

"Job changing or something, man?" Ryan asked, concerned.

Cole shook his head. "No, just curious what the place would bring, is all."

Ryan took the rambunctious puppy from Cole's lap when his friend was clearly not receptive to ten pounds of puppy spit on his hands and face. "It's Marie, isn't it?"

Cole nodded, looking straight into the fire. "She's it, man. If she'll have me, I'll see about selling and getting on with one of the outfits up near there."

"There can't be many jobs out that way," Ryan said, shocked.

"There are a few openings. I've been nosing around a little."

Ryan shook his head, but knew he couldn't truly judge. He'd move heaven and earth to be near Amy.

"Okay, man," he said, slapping Cole on the back. "I want to help pick the new neighbors," he said with a half grin. "Find us somebody with kids so mine have someone to play with."

"You bet, man. Might be nothing," Cole answered.

twenty-three

MARIE'S PHONE BUZZED ON HER desk loud enough to jolt Sally from her diatribe, and Marie gratefully took the chance to exit an endless conversation. "Sorry, Sally, I need to respond to this. Talk to you later," she said, turning her chair around and throwing up a prayer that poor Sally would get the social cue.

Party at my house Saturday night. Can you come? - Jesse

Marie was thankful because now she had a valid excuse to bug Holden. The phone rang five times before he answered.

"Holden? Hey, I wanted to know if we were on for lunch and an art show this weekend?"

He paused before answering. "Sorry, Mom. I've got plans with Dad this weekend."

All the air sucked out of the room at the utterance of that word. Marie felt her temper spike and had the sense to leave her cubicle and exit through the side door before responding. "Dad, is it now?" she asked, hearing the shrillness in her voice.

Holden stuttered a little. "Yeah, I mean, it feels weird to call him Kevin. He is my father, and father sounds too formal, so since it's weird anyway, I just thought…"

"Unbelievable."

"I'm sorry, Mom, it's just that. I'll drive on Saturday. We're going to the movies. I'm coming back to school Saturday night since I've got to study for a test on Monday." He paused. "I didn't think it would be that big of a deal."

She nodded and felt her cheeks glowing with disbelief and anger. She knew she had to tread carefully. If she flipped, Holden would continue not telling her everything, and that was driving her crazy.

"It's fine, Holden. I just don't like being left in the dark." At his pause, she continued, "Listen, I know you're an adult. I do worry about you, uh, interacting with Kevin, and I'd like to at least know your plans when he's involved. We don't know him, Holden."

"That's the thing. I'm trying to get to know him. I'm trying to at least give him a chance," Holden said defensively.

"Okay, son. Just be careful. Grandma's made other plans since I was waiting on you to finalize them, so I think I'm going to go to southern Illinois to see my friend Jesse. She's having a cookout and invited me."

"You're going down there a lot, huh?" he asked.

She decided Holden had enough on his plate with Kevin circling like a shark. She didn't want to add to the stress, so she left out the fact that she was considering moving there because she liked it so much.

"It's nice down there. Slow pace and friendly people. It's a nice change," Marie answered.

"Slow pace? Like you could deal with that, Mom," he said sarcastically.

"Well, I may not be buying cowboy boots or anything soon, but it feels homey there," she said. "Check in with me after you're back home on Saturday, so I can quit worrying?"

Holden sighed. "Okay. Love you."

"Love you." She disconnected the call and stared at Jesse's text.

Will Cole be there? - Marie

She watched the three little dots with a lump in her throat, waiting to see how Jesse was responding.

He has been invited. So has the guy that saved him. I figured the weather was starting to turn pretty, they're lucky to be alive, and we could use a good party, dang it! Everyone will be there. - Jesse

Sounds good to me. I miss him. - Marie

Wear something slutty. - Jesse

Shame on you! - Marie

I totally will. - Marie

Her friend was a mess, but maybe that's what she needed in her life. More fun. More celebrations. It certainly couldn't be as bad as the last get together. Marie took several deep breaths to be sure she was capable of plastering on a nice face for a few more hours until the workday was done.

MARIE TRIED NOT to make a face as the snick, snick, snick of tiny rocks clattered against the bottom of her car. She'd rolled down the windows to see if she could hear what was happening, but the stinky smell of tar caused her to quickly roll them right back up. Speeding up didn't help, but slowing down did.

"Oh my gosh, I thought I'd never get here. Something's wrong with your road!" Marie said as she met Jesse across the driveway when she pulled in.

"It's oil and chip, dummy. They just fixed the road," Jesse explained, taking the overnight bag from Marie.

Marie glared, completely unimpressed, as she stooped and picked off a few rocks from the panel of her car.

"You're going to need a solvent to get that tar off," a low voice rumbled from behind her.

Marie jolted up and shot a look at Jesse for not warning her that Cole was approaching. Jesse just grinned in the face of Marie's stink-eye and held her hand out to accept Marie's purse. Marie handed it over and walked over to Cole, who was hanging back a few feet.

"Hey, Cole," she said, as anxiousness filled her down to

her toes. She'd been preparing what to say to him for the two hours it took to drive here, but still, 'Hey, Cole," was the best she could do.

He took a step closer and held his hand out to her. She placed her hand in his and closed the distance between them. The arms that enveloped her felt so good. Marie let herself be held and absorbed his spicy, woodsy scent.

His hand slowly moved up her back to her neck as she leaned her head back. Cole half-smiled at her, but the smile didn't reach his eyes. Her hands went up to either side of his face.

"You didn't call," he said quietly.

"I'm sorry. I had to get my head on straight," Marie said. "How's your head?" she asked, turning his head so that she could see how he was doing. She ruffled his hair back to reveal a scar. "Gonna screw your hair up for good, isn't it?"

He grinned a little and ran his hand through it to rearrange what she had tussled. "Yeah, but that's okay. I wear a hat most of the time, anyway."

"Seriously, Cole, how are you? I mean, I've been keeping tabs on you through Jesse, but are you okay?"

"Keeping tabs on me, huh?" he asked, curiosity filled his gaze.

"Of course. I'm screwed up a little, but I'm not heartless," she answered matter-of-factly.

He laughed despite himself. "That's something I can understand. Come on, let's go get a drink."

Marie allowed Cole to lead her to the house. She

looped her arm around his waist as they made it into the large kitchen, where the familiar faces were gathered. She distributed hugs to women and nods to the men, whom she didn't know as well.

"This is my husband, Jake," Avery volunteered, as she realized they hadn't met yet. A weight threatened to settle in Marie's stomach as she remembered that Jake had hauled Cole off in handcuffs at the last gathering.

"And this," Cole said as he pulled an even bigger man to his side in a one-armed hug, "is Big Daddy Don. He's the reason I'm even here tonight."

"Aw, hell, son. I hate when you call me that," Don said, darting his eyes in embarrassment to a pretty older woman in the kitchen.

With a goofy smile on her face, Marie held her hand out to introduce herself properly but hesitated awkwardly when she realized Don's arm was in a cast.

"Nice to meet you, Big Daddy Don," she said, clasping his good arm in greeting.

Jesse stepped forward. "Marie, this is my mom, Eadie. I'm not sure if you two have met yet or not," she said, as the woman walked up and wrapped Marie in a hug.

"So nice to meet you, dear. My, your hair is beautiful! I love the curls! Are you Italian?" Eadie asked.

"Mom, you're not supposed to ask stuff like that anymore," Jesse said, rolling her eyes.

"What? Some of my favorite TV chefs are Italian! Have you seen the one with her boobs hiked up to her chin?

I don't approve of her outfits, but her recipes are delicious and she has the prettiest smile!" Eadie said, causing Don to smother a laugh with a cough.

Jesse bugged out her eyes, and Marie couldn't help but laugh. Eadie was younger than her mother, but they were going to get along well.

"Did Jesse tell me you were moving down here, Marie?" Eadie asked, causing a silence to settle in the chaotic kitchen. The only sounds were the kids arguing in the family room over which music to play next.

"Uh," she faltered, "I am thinking about it." Marie shot a look at Jesse who was wild-eyed. Clearly, she'd spilled the beans to her mother and forgot to mention it was a secret.

Cole went stiff as a board against Marie's side. She glanced up at him but couldn't read his impassive expression. She swallowed and cussed to herself. She'd planned to see how tonight went before making her plans known.

Mallory read the room and tried to create a distraction by crooning about all the desserts Eadie and Ruthie had made for the gathering, each one more delicious looking than the next. The group shifted their focus, and Jesse mouthed "sorry" from across the room.

Marie took Cole's hand and squeezed it. "Can we talk somewhere?" she whispered.

He nodded and walked her through the kitchen to a back porch where a raging bonfire had been built to warm anyone brave enough to venture out into the cool evening weather. He didn't say anything, but took a drink of the beer he'd picked up in the kitchen.

Marie did the same before spitting her words out. "I wasn't going to say anything tonight, obviously…"

"Obviously, because you didn't talk to me at all over the past three weeks," he added bitterly.

"Fine, I deserved that. Here's something I need you to understand, Cole. I don't typically *do* relationships. I've made that pretty clear, right? So, if I'm interested enough to take a leap of faith for someone, it scares the living heck out of me. I'm not some twenty-year-old who can make a move and chalk it up to a 'life lesson' if it craps out. I need to think things through. I've got a grown son, an elderly mother, and a career to maneuver around, so just give me a freaking minute if I need time to think," she said, stopping herself from poking him in the chest to make her point.

He put his hands up a little. "Marie, I know. I've already made it clear how I feel. I'll tell you something, since we're swapping life truths here," he said, as he looked around like he couldn't believe they were having such an important conversation on Jesse and Levi's porch. "I've only been in love one other time in my life. It was a disaster. This scares me, too. You might need me to 'give you a freaking minute,' but I need you to talk to me. There's got to be some kind of compromise in this thing, or it's going to end before it gets started." He pulled her closer. "I want you, and I need to know what you're thinking when it comes to us."

"Are we fighting or making up here?" she asked as worry wrinkled her brow.

He leaned forward to kiss her forehead. "I don't know.

A little of both," he said, tipping his head down to her neck and placing a kiss on her skin.

Her head automatically tipped back, and Cole took advantage of the access to her lips. He smiled and pulled her close at the end of their kiss, and she enjoyed leaning into his chest. A low laugh escaped him.

"What?" she asked, pulling back to look in his eyes.

"We're not the only ones hitting it off tonight," he said, turning her shoulders so that she could peek into the glass doors from their spot on the corner of the deck. Don and Eadie were shoulder to shoulder, deep in discussion over the dessert offerings.

"Well that's the cutest thing I've ever seen," Marie said.

"It is, isn't it?" Cole said. "Let's go in. You're shivering."

"I don't think it's the weather," she said.

"Grab your bag that Jesse took, Marie. Come stay with me tonight," he said with hope.

She held his sultry gaze for a minute and raised an eyebrow. "Fine. Stay for ten more minutes?"

He glanced at his watch as if he were afraid they'd stay one minute more than necessary. "Fine." He grinned.

twenty-four

"**H**OLDEN, I'M SO GLAD you took the news so well," she said to her son, relieved to finally have him within arm's reach again.

"Mom, it's not that big of a deal," he said with a shrug. "I have some news of my own…"

Marie tilted her head, willing him to spit it out. At his silence, she gestured for him to speak. "Spit it out, son, I'm dying here!"

Holden took off his hat and raked his hand through his hair, the same way he'd done since he was a small boy. "I landed an internship in Chicago. At that firm I told you about. The really big one," he said with a giant smile.

Marie felt stunned—momentarily pinned between

elated and terrified. Her boy was watching her with those big eyes, and she had to react perfectly. She smiled from ear to ear and threw her hands as wide as she could make them. Holden grabbed her in a hug, and she held him as tight as she could, sniffing in that neck smell that all moms know from the very core of their being. Tears filled her eyes, and she did her best to keep them at bay.

"Oh crap, Mom, are you crying?" Holden asked, eyes as big as saucers.

"Kid, I'm so darned proud of you I could just die. That internship was really competitive, wasn't it? I knew you could do it!" Marie leaned in and listened as Holden rehashed the hoops he had to jump through during the application process and what his internship would entail. Marie nearly bit off her own tongue as she fought to not give a voice to all the fears she had of her son moving to a new city. *He is a good boy—a fine young man*, she amended. *He is going to do well for himself.*

Mentally, she calculated the days he had left of school, and her heart lodged in her throat. "Holden, when do you leave for Chicago?"

He pulled a face, and Marie knew she wasn't going to like his answer. "I move the day after graduation. I'm going up next weekend to find an apartment."

Marie heaved a sigh. She had hoped to have him home for a few weeks at least. Then she remembered she had her own relocation to manage. "This whole growing up thing sucks, son. It went too quickly."

"It's okay, Mom. At least we'll be in the same state, right? And, here, let me calculate the distance," he said, fishing in his pocket for his phone.

Marie looked at her watch, surprised that Cole was late. He was supposed to meet them for lunch so that he could be properly introduced to Holden, this time without the headlock. If Marie was going to consider dating him, she needed this addressed and over with.

"See? It's five hours from St. Louis to Chicago, and after you move to Illinois, you'll just be one more hour away. It's still driveable in a day," Holden said. "What?" he asked, wiping at his face. "Got something on me?"

She shook her head. "No, son. It's just remarkable how you can still look just like you did as a little boy one minute, and completely grown the next. The stubble helps," she said, scratching at his cheek. He twisted his head away from her and laughed. His expression changed when he saw Marie's mouth drop open. He jerked his gaze in the direction hers had taken, and his face echoed hers. Kevin was storming toward their table at a clipped pace.

Marie stood at his approach, placing herself in front of Holden.

"Sit down, bitch. I'm here to talk to him, not you," Kevin said, jerking his thumb in Holden's direction.

Holden pushed in front of Marie in an instant. "Dad, don't talk to her like that!" he said, lowering his voice at the end. "We're in public. If you want to talk, then sit down, but you can't stay if you talk to her like that."

Marie looked between the two men, in awe of how much they favored each other. Kevin was taller than Holden, and his frame more wiry, but the faces were structured the same. Holden had her mop of dark, curly hair, but even his hairline matched Kevin's. Her pulse had kicked up so hard that she would've sworn she could hear her heartbeat in her ears. She gave herself a shake, needing to focus on what was being said.

Kevin jerked a chair back from the table and sat down heavily. "The only reason I'm letting you get away with speaking to me that way is because we are in public, son. You do it again, and you'll get my fist through your teeth."

"I see you're the same son of a bitch you used to be," Marie hissed. "Say what you need to say and get out of here."

Kevin barely spared her a glance. "I'm not here to talk to you. You're dead to me. You kept Holden from me long enough. I finally got him, and now he's leaving for Chicago? How am I supposed to get to you there? I can't go further than fifty miles without permission from my parole officer. Chicago?" he asked, his voice hitching at the end of his question as he shook his head.

"And, to make it worse, you tell me this in a text message?" he asked, his glassy eyes hardening into a glare as he looked at his son. "Not even a real phone call?"

Holden shrugged. "I didn't think how I told you would matter. I thought you'd be excited for me."

Kevin shook his head in disgust as he looked down at the table.

"I don't remember telling you I was meeting Mom today," Holden asked, tilting his head and leaning back in his chair. "How did you know I was here?"

"Tracker," Kevin answered, looking directly into Holden's eyes.

"Huh?" Holden asked, confused.

"Track-er," he answered, dragging out the word slowly as he tapped his finger on the phone Holden had laid on the table. Marie's stomach flipped at the memory of hearing the same tone in his voice when he would come home wasted and ready for an argument. She sniffed in Kevin's direction and recoiled.

She leaned closer to Holden and, in a quiet voice, said, "He's drunk."

"I told you to shut up, Marie," Kevin said, hatred in his voice. "You never could follow directions."

She looked up at him in embarrassment for her son, and behind Kevin's shoulder, she saw Cole approaching across the plaza. *Hells bells. Here we go*, she thought. She had forgotten about Cole in the chaos of Kevin's arrival.

He smiled as he spotted them and threw up a hand in a wave. She managed a fake smile, lifted her hand quickly to return the wave, and wished the ground would open up and swallow Kevin whole.

"Hells bells," Holden said quietly, reflecting Marie's sentiment.

Kevin's head spun around and took in the approaching figure before he turned back to Marie. "Ah, what's this?"

he said sarcastically. "Is this…" he looked back to Cole and then Marie, "is this some kind of little new family reunion or something? Well, hot dog! I'm so glad I'm here for it."

Marie stood up when Kevin sprang from his chair and turned to face Cole. She watched as Cole's whole demeanor changed from excited to defensive. His stride lengthened, his hands closed at his sides, and it almost seemed like he grew taller. He looked from the stranger to Marie, and back as he arrived at the table.

"Well, hello, and who the hell are you?" Kevin asked Cole.

Cole looked from the man's face to Marie. "Marie, is everything alright?" he asked with a grim set to his mouth. His eyes traveled to Holden, and he gave a slight nod in greeting, which Holden returned.

Kevin huffed in exasperation. "You're not even going to speak to me, huh? Real manly," he said, then turned to Marie. "Guess your taste in men deteriorated after me."

In the second it took Marie to jump from her seat, Holden had placed himself in front of Marie, and Cole was so close to Kevin, it's a wonder they didn't share the same skin.

"I think you've said enough for today, don't you?" Cole asked, looking down at Kevin with a glare that would make a sober man wither.

Kevin looked up as Cole stood motionless, his face unchanging as he debated his next step. Whatever he saw in Cole's eyes was enough to cause him to resist whatever he was about to say next. He stubbornly stayed in place.

Marie wondered if Kevin thought Cole would back up and adhere to the social norms that made this kind of animalistic, threatening behavior a no-go for *normal* people. She reached over and took Holden's hand in hers, and he gave it a quick squeeze. Anxiety rolled off him, and he broke the silence first.

"Dad, I think you should go. I'll call you later, and we can talk more about Chicago, okay?" Holden said, slicing Marie's heart in two. Her boy was an eternal peacemaker, the counterbalance to her own aggressive personality.

At the sound of Holden's voice, the challenge seemed to die out of Kevin, and he took a step back from Cole. Cole didn't move an inch and stood ready to beat Kevin into a bloody pulp if he so much as flinched in the wrong direction.

Kevin shook his head slowly and looked at Holden. "You're not going anywhere. Screw Chicago." He took a few steps and turned back to shove the chair back under the table. Metal scraped against the concrete patio. Kevin shook his head from side to side as if he were arguing with himself, and he stepped back and turned toward the patio exit.

Cole stayed standing as Kevin walked out of the exit and made his way through the plaza as he dodged some people and intentionally bumped into others. When he appeared to have cleared the area, Cole turned back to Marie and Holden. "You guys okay?" he asked as he stepped closer to Marie and pulled her into a hug. She nodded, unable to speak. Cole held out a hand to Holden. "Hey, man."

Holden uttered, "Hey," and exhaled the breath that had been lodged in his throat as he watched his father exit.

"That," she gestured, "was my ex." She made a pinched face when she noticed her hands were trembling. "Son, has he ever acted like that in front of you? Surely, you wouldn't meet with—"

"No," Holden answered and interrupted her. "No way. If he had acted that way, I'd never have seen him again. I didn't think..." he said as his voice trailed off and he shook his head.

Cole cleared his voice and pulled out the chair that Kevin had vacated to the side of the table where he could keep an eye on the people milling around. "Uh, I'm not sure this is the best timing, considering what just happened, but I wanted to apologize to you for what I did the last time we met," he said, looking Holden in the eye.

"It's cool, man," Holden said. "I mean, don't ever do it again, but we're cool." Holden's hands automatically went to his neck as he turned it to each side to loosen the muscles tensed from what had just transpired.

Cole gave him a nod. Marie exhaled and took a drink from her water glass. "I can't believe that just happened. Holden was just telling me about landing the internship of his dreams, and Kevin showed up, ready to fight or something. Drunk as a skunk, no less."

"Yeah, picked up on that," Cole said, wiping at his nose with his hand. "Congrats on the internship."

Marie picked up the menu and Cole put his hand on

hers. "I'm sorry I was late. The traffic was backed up coming over the bridge. I didn't expect it would be so rough today."

"Ballgame," Marie and Holden said at the same time, which caused Marie to smile.

"That'll be a big change," Holden said to Marie. "No traffic?" he clarified for Marie who looked confused. "Didn't you say that town was pretty small?"

She laughed. "Oh yeah. It'll take some getting used to, but I think I'll like it. Finally, I got to meet with my boss. He's okay with me coming in once every two weeks instead of weekly and confirmed I'll keep the Midwest territory, so other than taking longer to get to an airport, nothing changes there."

"What did Grandma think of her housing options?" Holden asked, concerned.

Marie shrugged. "It's the craziest thing. She doesn't seem ruffled about it at all. There's a retirement community in the same town where I'll be, and a bigger one in the next town over. She's leaning toward that one. It's close to Target, and Target has Starbucks."

Holden nodded. "That would do it for me. She's pretty serious about her frappuccinos."

"I'm glad you could come up," she said to Cole, reaching over to squeeze his arm.

His lips lifted in a smile. "Me, too. You saved me a lot of trouble, you know."

Marie's brow wrinkled. "What do you mean?"

Cole leaned back, stretched his legs out, and crossed

his ankles, drawing out the moment. "Well, I'd made some calls about a transfer. Had an appraiser come check out the house and land to give me a sale price."

Her eyebrows show up to her hairline. "What?" she asked, too loud for their surroundings.

Holden laughed and Cole smiled. "Yup."

"You were going to sell that amazing house, and what? Move here?" she asked, shocked.

He nodded, and she shook her head from side to side as her fingers raked through the curls before she tied it up in a ponytail with an elastic from her wrist.

"No way. You'd hate it up here."

"Well, if it was the only way I was going to get to see you, it would've been worth it."

She couldn't believe her ears. "I can't see you schlepping through traffic jams every day. Or waking up surrounded by people instead of trees. No way. You'd go bananas."

He lifted a shoulder. "Probably, but it would be worth it. Glad you beat me to the punch, though."

"Happy to be of service," she said sarcastically.

Holden stood. "Excuse me. Be back in a few," he said, before he walked the short distance to the restaurant entrance to use the facilities.

Marie leaned over to plant a warm, soft kiss on Cole's lips. "I'm so glad you showed up when you did. That scared the living daylights out of me. I can't believe Kevin behaved like that in front of Holden. I knew he was hateful and abusive, but I wouldn't have guessed he'd have a screw totally loose.

I mean, who threatens someone like that? Especially over something like Holden getting an internship. If he'd done something bad, maybe, but dang. He's living his dream; it's a good thing."

Cole nodded, happy to have her close. His fingers moved to the back of her neck, and he pulled her close for one more kiss when he heard heavy footsteps. He looked out to the plaza to see Kevin walking quickly back to their table. Alarms went off in his mind as he shoved Marie back down to her chair and leapt to his feet. He watched Kevin take in Holden's empty seat, and a lead weight settled in his gut as the man's erratic emotions played on his face.

From the corner of his eye, he saw Holden resurface at the restaurant entrance. Instantly, Cole spread his arms out wide and ran to Holden as he bellowed, "Get down!"

Marie watched in horror as Kevin reached in the back of his waist and pulled out a gun, and took aim at Holden.

Kevin's face contorted in rage and he screamed, "Son, you are not ever leaving me again!" He pulled the trigger as Cole reached Holden. Cole threw his own body over the boy's, and Holden smashed back into the door he just walked through.

The bullet ripped into Cole's chest, and he sagged back as Marie's screams filled the air. People screamed and ran, flipping over chairs as they scrambled for safety. Two more shots resonated, and Kevin dropped to the ground, his leg shattered by two bullets. An older man stood nearby, weapon drawn. Completely unassuming in his golf shirt and khaki shorts, the gray-haired fellow kept his gun trained on Kevin as he advanced and barked an order. "Slide your weapon away from you right now, you son of a bitch!" the man yelled. "I been watching you make a fool of yourself with these nice people, and by God, I'm not going to sit here while you hurt anybody else today."

"Jesus Christ, Bill!" the man's friend said when he walked back to the man. "I didn't even know you had a gun on you!"

Bill turned his head and addressed his friend in exasperation, "I'm from Orlando; everybody carries a gun!"

The instant Kevin was on the ground, Marie ran to the doorway where Holden held his T-shirt against the hole in Cole's chest. She searched all over Holden for injuries as she knelt beside Cole. Her trembling hands went to his blood-soaked shirt as if she could will the spreading stains away. "Cole," she whispered his name like a prayer and cupped his face in her hands.

His eyes were hard, but he tried to turn the corners of his mouth up.

"No, don't try and make me feel better," she said with a forced smile. "You're going to be okay, Cole. You're going to be okay." Marie looked up into Holden's huge eyes, and she was gutted by the horror she found there. "Holden?" Using her Mom voice, she said his name in a way that asked all the questions she was terrified to vocalize at the moment.

Holden understood. "I'm fine, Mom," he said with a blink. He relented as Marie put her hands on his to take over holding pressure on Cole's wound.

"I called nine one one!" a waitress shouted over the noise of people trying to file out the patio door and rerouting to the front door. "Here, honey," the waitress said, handing Holden a t-shirt with their pub logo on it to replace the one he used to staunch Cole's bleeding.

Everything from the moment she got to Holden and Cole happened in slow motion for Marie. Plaza security was followed closely by police. Sirens blared in the air, and feet trampled all around as Marie knelt at Cole's side. An officer took over holding the pressure on Cole's chest until the paramedics arrived. Marie's phone blew up with coworkers checking on her. They'd heard gunshots near her office building, and they knew she was there with her son.

Kevin was scraped from the sidewalk, and officers questioned the man who had shot him. News cameras arrived and reported what they were able to gather in different corners of the scene. Marie vaguely registered the thought that she should call her mother to let her know what happened before she caught it on the news, but that would have to wait.

"It's going to be okay," Marie said, sliding into the ambulance beside Cole, who had been loaded onto a stretcher and given an oxygen mask.

"Holden?" he asked as he pulled the mask from his face.

"You need to keep that in place, sir," the EMT said to Cole, not flinching at the withering look Cole shot him.

Marie choked on the sob that threatened to escape. "He's fine. You saved…" her voice broke off. "You saved him, Cole.

He's following us to the hospital." She wiped her nose with her wrist since her hands were soaked in his blood. Cole's complexion was a ghostly pale, and she was terrified. "He's so pale," she said to the EMT.

"The bullet went all the way through, ma'am. He was still bleeding from the back when he was on the ground. He's lost a lot of blood, but we're almost to the hospital," the young man answered.

Marie nodded and turned her attention back to Cole. "You're going to be fine," she crooned as she leaned over to kiss his sweat-soaked forehead.

Within minutes of arriving at the hospital, Cole was whisked off to surgery while Marie filled out what paperwork she could with shaking hands. A nurse had shown her to a restroom so that she could wash up. When she made it back to the lobby, Holden was there and had gathered coffee and water.

The last hour added years to Holden's handsome face. "I didn't know which one you'd want, so I grabbed both," he said quietly.

Marie gathered him into a hug and squeezed. "Honey, I'm so sorry. I'm so sorry for what your father did—for what he tried to do," she said, fresh tears springing to her eyes.

He shook his head. "I can't believe this, Mom. He was going to kill me. I can't believe he was that dangerous, and I was oblivious. I mean, I knew he was intense and creepy, but I didn't think…" he said, his voice trailing off. He put his head on hers and let himself be hugged for longer than he normally allowed.

She patted him and withdrew. "That little feeling in your gut when you're with someone, you can't ignore that. I think you wanted him to be decent so badly that maybe it was hard to pay attention to that feeling." She eased into a seat and took the cup of coffee.

Holden sank down in the next chair, and to Marie's surprise, he didn't pull out his phone. Instead, he leaned his head back against the wall and closed his eyes. Suddenly, she jerked in her chair.

"Mom?" Holden asked, staring at her.

Frantically, she fished her phone from her purse. "I forgot to call Grandma!"

On the first ring, her mother answered. "Well, thank God. I was scared to death!" she yelled into the phone. "What happened, Marie? Isn't this your day in the office? Did you see anything?"

Marie stood, bracing herself against the torrent of questions, and the reaction she knew was coming. She gave Holden's hand a squeeze and tilted her head toward the door. "I'm going to step outside to talk to Gram. Come get me if you hear anything, okay?"

It took nearly everything she had to leave his side, but there was no way she was going recount the details with Holden sitting next to her. It was bad enough that scene would forever be burned into his memory. *This is going to screw him up*, she worried to herself.

True to form, Marie's mother had come apart at the news. She would have preferred to tell her everything in person, but she wasn't leaving Cole. Marie soaked in every ray of the bright sunlight as she gathered her wits before going back into the hospital. Her mother's voice rang in her ears. *"He stepped in front of a gun to protect Holden?"* she had said in reverence. *"Marie, honey, you marry that man, or I'll marry him myself."*

"I couldn't have said it better myself, Mom. I will if he'll have me," Marie vowed.

epilogue

"You're going to wear a path on the wood floor," Cole teased, pulling Marie close to his side.

She leaned into him for about six seconds before separating to continue her path. On the next circuit she raised on her tiptoes to whisper in his ear, "The people just keep coming!" Her eyes were wide, and she'd pulled her hair back to keep the tendrils from circling her face.

"I talked to Kelly this morning. She and the kids will be here in a few hours. She had to finish up a project at work."

Marie nodded. "I'm glad Holden will get to meet them. I can't believe it's time for him to move already." He reached up to tuck an errant curl behind her ear and winced, which did not escape her notice. "Did you remember to take your pain pill?" she asked, checking her watch.

"Might've forgotten about that last one. I don't like taking that crap," he whined.

Her head shook in endearing annoyance. "Yes, but you've had three surgeries in as many months. You need to be patient with yourself. You're a caveman, not Superman," she said with a sigh as she plucked the bottle from the cabinet and held it out to him.

He accepted the bottle and raised his fingers in mock surrender. "Yes, ma'am, you're the boss," he said with an indulgent smile.

The light tone of his voice paired with his blue-green eyes helped ease the nervousness in her stomach. She resumed her spot by his side and watched as people filled his home. "Thanks for letting us have Holden's going away party here. I can't believe some of his friends came from the city. Some of them have never even been out in the country like this. Look at them, it's like they're in a different world."

"Funny how some people can be so sheltered, huh?" he said with a sneaky grin.

When it registered with her that he was making fun of how long it took her to acclimate to country life, she blushed and laughed.

Jesse blew into the kitchen like a tornado with five kids trailing behind her, all with covered dishes. "What are you two doing in here, hiding? Hey, Cole, is it okay if Levi takes the charcoal straight to the back? He cut around the side of the house."

"Sure, glad you guys could make it," he said with a smile.

Marie stepped away from Cole's side and took the steaming dish from Jesse's hands. "Here, let me help. Oooh, Jesse! What is this? It smells amazing!"

Cole greeted the kids congregating in the living room and placed a peck on Marie's cheek on his way out the door. "I'm going to go man the grill."

"What is it with men and fire?" Marie asked Jesse.

"No idea, but they can keep the grill. I could eat this whole pan. This," Jesse crowed, "is my secret recipe... Slap Your Mama Chicken Stuffing Casserole," she said, waggling her eyebrows.

"Oh my gosh, is that butter I smell?" Marie moaned.

"So much butter. Don't even ask," she teased, pulling out pot holders from a drawer after opening several. "This is beautiful, by the way," Jesse said, pulling Marie's left hand into clear view. The engagement ring sparkled in the light. "Nicely done, Cole," she teased to the empty space where he had been standing minutes ago.

Marie grinned from ear to ear. "Thank you. I love it." She leaned forward and whispered in Jesse's ear as people milled in and out of the room grabbing peeks at what goodies there were to eat. "How do you enjoy throwing parties? It's making me insane."

She shrugged. "I love it—the chaos, kids, music, the food! What's not to love?"

"The chaos, kids, music, and food. Next one's at your house then, you win," Marie said, helping Jesse arrange dishes on the counter.

"Hey, I offered!" Jesse argued, stinging Marie with her stink-eye.

"You know me, I have to be in charge. You can do it next time, though."

"You? Bossy?" Jesse teased.

Marie shrugged. "I am what I am! Thank God he likes it," Marie said with a laugh, gesturing toward the deck. Through the wall of windows, the women watched as the men all gathered around the grill.

"Sometimes it all just works," Jesse said, pulling her friend in for a quick hug.

The door opened and Mallory walked in with a tray of cookies. "Take these from me before I eat more of them," she lamented, rubbing a hand over her rounded belly.

Instantly, Jesse and Marie had their hands on her stomach. "You people are the only ones I let do this. You know that, right?" Mallory asked in her less-than-enthused voice.

"Oh, stop being so crabby. Here, have another cookie. Why don't you go put your feet up in the living room?" Jesse fussed.

Mallory tilted to the side and examined her swollen ankles. "Stuff like this is funny when it happens to other women," she mused, placing her hands at the bottom of her stomach. "I even have to kind of lift everything up when I go pee. Baby A's head is kinking the line or something. And Baby B," she said, rubbing the top of her belly under her ribs, "is keeping me from eating as much as I want. I'm so hungry, but I fill up so fast!" she whined.

"Twin girls," Marie mused. "You're going to have so much fun, Mal."

Avery entered the kitchen with bottles of wine in each hand. "Hey, all." She leaned in to collect hugs from the ladies. "What are we talking about?"

"Twins," Mallory answered. "I still can't believe it. For a week, all we did was say 'twins' to each other at random times." A bemused expression filled her lovely face. "You should've seen Cade's face when they said two girls. He went as pale as a ghost. The day after, he said, 'Oh my God, the shoes...' like he was in a trance. I think he's envisioning dollar bills flying out the door."

Avery pulled Mallory into a one-armed hug. "Don't even tell him about prom dresses. He's a big boy. He can handle it." She laughed.

"Aw, babe. Bragging about me again?" Jake asked as he entered the kitchen and dodged Jesse's swat.

"Gross, get a room." Mallory groaned.

His eyebrows waggled at the suggestion. "Not here. Go home," Marie said, eyes to the ceiling.

"Fine, thirty minutes?" Jake asked Avery as a lascivious smile lit up his face.

Mallory leaned against a counter. "Yuck, no sister wants to picture her brother getting it on."

Jake cackled. "What, those twins of yours occurred from immaculate conception or something?"

Marie leaned against Avery's hug and laughed. "You guys are a mess. Hey, where's Toby?" Marie asked Avery, scanning the open layout to find their sweet, adopted son. Of all the kids in the gaggle of people, Toby was her favorite.

Avery pulled out her phone to check for missed messages. He's at Ruthie's tonight. She and Hank are keeping him and Benji. They're headed to the movies. I imagine they'll be totally overfed on sugar and popcorn, but they're sleeping over with them tonight, so I'm officially off the clock," she said somewhat anxiously.

"Us, too!" Anna said as Avery jumped.

She placed her hand over hear heart. "Good grief, Anna, I didn't even see you come in."

"Sorry!" she said, fanning her hands out in front of her. "We haven't had a night off in forever," Anna said, wrapping her husband Aidan in hug as he balanced a pie.

"I'm surprised Mom didn't watch Benji," Jesse said as she plucked the pie from Aidan's hand.

"Mom's busy," Anna said conspiratorially. Jesse spun around with big eyes, desperate for details. "She's on a date!"

Jesse's hoot of excitement filled the room, drawing the attention of the kids crowded around the big TV in the living room. A chorus of "whats" sounded from the room, ignored by the women.

"Shh! Grown-ups are talking!" Jake said in falsetto as he and Aidan left to join the men out back.

Anna nodded her head. "It's true! Remember Don?" Jesse's brow wrinkled in confusion.

"Don?" Marie questioned. "You mean Cole's friend? The one that pushed him out of the way when the tree fell?"

"Yes! That's the one! Apparently he swapped numbers with Mom at the last party, and they've been talking on the phone!" Anna's eyes were filled with happiness, and Jesse's grew wet with tears.

Jesse grabbed Anna for a quick hug. "Dad would want that, wouldn't he?" Jesse asked Anna quietly. Anna nodded. Eadie, their mother, had been so lonesome during the years since he had died. Their father would have wanted Eadie to find a friend and keep joy in her life.

"Maybe she can go on a double date with my mom." Marie cackled. "Do they play shuffleboard or bowl, maybe?"

All heads turned to Marie. "I'm not joking. She found herself a feller. Competition is steep in the retirement village, but she's a tough old bird."

Marie laughed and realized she was fully enjoying the moment. Their home on Eagle Mountain glowed with light and was literally filled with laughter. She watched through the windows as Holden stood next to the man she loved. By the way Cole gestured to one of the hulking pines that surrounded the deck, he was explaining something about the trees, and the young men listened with interest. The sunset was on full display from their perch on the mountain, and a happy feeling settled in her soul. *So much for a quick cabin getaway*, she joked to herself. She drew a deep breath and soaked it all in. Maybe one of life's biggest blessings was getting what you didn't know you always wanted.

acknowledgements

I would like to first thank my family for their willingness to listen to my crazy story ideas and for always offering creative suggestions of their own. Their creativity and energy inspires me daily.

My friends deserve a round of applause for not rolling their eyes when I grab my phone mid-conversation to note down whatever wild thing they just said. Sorry ladies, some of that material is just too good not to use. Really, it's a small price to pay for my unwavering friendship, right?

Eagle Mountain has already had a lot of love from friends and family, and I am very thankful. First up, thank you to my friends and beta readers for jumping in to point out trouble spots in my rough draft: Angie Clifton, Sarah Hart, Jerri Harbison, Regina Murphy, and Julie Natzke. Yet again, the hero of my story worked in a field I knew nothing about, so thank you to Tyler Van Ormer and Aaron Moore for sharing information about forestry and to Erin Fritz for sharing information about medical protocol.

Sarah West at Three Owls Editing, you have the patience of a saint. Thank you for tolerating me as I watch your cursor like a hawk. It's thrilling to watch you catch errors that I missed after staring at this baby for hours and hours.

Cassy Roop at Pink Ink Designs, you are a wizard at cover design and formatting. You've done such an amazing job making all four covers in the Coal Country Series blend together perfectly, and your interior formatting is always beautiful.

To my author friends, thank you for fielding a million questions and offering your friendship. Anne Conley, Erica Cope, Autumn Doughton, Hazel James, and Stacy Kestwick, I consider you all creative geniuses and masterful storytellers. It's awfully special to discover that you're friendly and helpful, to boot.

Bloggers and Bookstagrammers, thank you for sharing your favorite stories with your readers. Your support and enthusiasm make the difference between an author writing a great story and sharing a great story with the world. Thank you for helping get much-loved books in the hands of much-loved readers.

To the readers who have come to love the characters in the Coal Country Series, I hope you love this story! I've been dying to get back to Cole since the ending of *Fishing Hole*, and I thank you for your continued love and support. Your reviews help bring visibility to the series, and I hope you enjoy the continuity of the characters. Your support, comments, and recommendations to friends are so appreciated. Thank you for helping make my dream a reality!

More by Hillary DeVisser

If you enjoyed this story, please consider writing a review on Amazon and Goodreads.com. Thank you for taking the time to read my book. I hope you loved it!

Also, you might enjoy my other books in the Coal Country Series:

Fishing Hole
Copper Creek
Poets Pass

CPSIA information can be obtained
at www.ICGtesting.com
Printed in the USA
LVHW021222071019
633402LV00002B/452/P